The Persimmon Trail
& other stories

JUYANNE JAMES

FALL 2015

BROKEN LEVEE BOOKS / An imprint of Chin Music Press
SEATTLE

The Persimmon Trail
& other stories

Contents

You Don't Know Me, Child

The first time I saw her was at a bus stop in New Orleans. I had been attending a class on African American history, and my mind was fresh with images of sturdy Africans at Congo Square, many of them just off slave boats. I could still feel the pain of the mothers who'd had their babies pried from their arms. There had been so much loss back then that I could only imagine how they'd survived. As I sat there on the bus, looking out at this woman, it seemed wholly possible that she had jumped from the pages of our history textbook.

To me, she seemed injured and embattled; she held dark secrets I wanted to learn about. Her skin was just black, like mine, but hers was shiny like minuscule specks of copper flecked through her. She was of the earth, its flesh and blood. I fell instantly in love with the crown of pictures, which she wore upon her head. I began to imagine how she had come about those honorable associations: there was a picture of Jesus—in some other life she could have walked side by side with Him, both of them sandal-footed, him teaching and preaching along the road to Galilee. I imagined her later, offering him water to drink as he dragged his cross up the hill. There was Obama, too, his photo tucked behind Martin's, like one could not supplant the other. I thought, there must be a small photo of Rosa Parks in there, somewhere, although it was not apparent. As the woman turned her head, slightly, I saw what looked like old black and white photos of Freedom Riders. Her proud look could have placed her back then. Some of the photos were attached with safety pins and paper clips, others sewn into her hair with various colors of thread. It was as safe a place to keep them as any other—it seemed to me that she could not afford to lose those pictures.

As the long line of passengers continued to board the bus, the woman didn't make a move to get aboard. Instead, she stood up and held out both hands, cupped, as though she were waiting for someone to fill them running over. Her eyes found me staring. It would have been good of me to turn away, but I couldn't. I was mesmerized, you see.

Upon noticing me, the woman moved quickly from the small bench. She was suddenly at me, as she threw herself against the side of the bus. The bus rocked like it was floating in water. Her crown of photos was then reversed. There were no more icons—no new presidents or the King of Kings, nor King himself—just the oval snapshot of a small child, its chubby cheeks smashed against the bus window. The eyes were minute coins of silver, for the picture was faded. Or was it that the bus, now sweaty with its new passengers, was pulling away, and I could no longer see the picture clearly? It was obvious that this one photo held a special resting place on her crown. I couldn't help but wonder who the child could have been—was the toddler long dead, or taken away from her, or in some other way horribly missing from the woman's life?

She stepped back from the curb, and while still looking at me, she coughed up from the dark pit of her belly a heavy glob of spit which she spat in my direction. The window was closed, but instinctively my body fell back, my face not wanting to taste the anger that she had thrown. I looked down at my skin; I had now become the brighter berry. The sun had used the spit like a prism and coated my arm in a stunning lightness. I didn't know what to say, how to react to this, to her. I wished my eyes could convey to her how connected she and I must be, as fellow travelers on this difficult ride through life. But as the bus pulled away, I could hear her say, "You don't know me." She repeated the words, in a slower, guttural refrain, "You don't know me, child."

Whenever I rode the bus, I would look for the woman at the bus stop. Sometimes she was actually on the bus, acting as her own type of freedom rider, as she spit out her contempt for almost everything that she saw. Once, I saw her attempt to throw a curse on CP3, or at least his image. As we rounded the HOV lane and there was Chris Paul's larger than life face pasted to the side of New Orleans Arena, she crossed her fingers and pointed at him. Then with an index finger and ring finger, she touched her eyes and pointed again, as she said, "I see you." She repeated those words, too: "I see you."

Most of the people on the bus who had noticed her actions turned and shot disconcerted glances at each other. I heard one of the elderly bus riders say, "Oh, Lord, another Katrina survivor," and everyone who heard this understood how the great storm had changed people like her. I could see this woman and women like her being rescued from the tops of cars, vans, or even buses—the flood waters eating all around them. Had her child fallen off, or slipped away in the night as the mother drew in a minute of slumber? I could suddenly see why the picture was faded—how much water the woman must have carried her belongings through. How soon the baby's picture would have been saturated—not only in the flood waters but in the woman's tears as well.

I looked again at her, standing in the aisle at the front of the bus. The woman was staring back at me. I almost expected her to throw another glob of spit at me. But this time her eyes were calm, as if she recognized the pain of remembrance in my face.

I have not seen her lately. The African American history class ended two years ago, and I have now graduated from college. Often, I think back to the first time I saw her at that bus stop on Canal Street. Even though she spat at me, I was fascinated by her—or was it the lives I imagined she had lived? I now know it was more than that. She connected me to my past in a way that a mere textbook could not. Her sadness reached over to me, tapped me on the shoulder, and made me take notice—teaching me always to be respectful and careful, and to hold on to people at all costs, particularly those who have left this world.

The woman is the obvious damaged soul, but I know that I am damaged, too. We all are. I hope the history books will one day tell the world just how much we lost.

The Wicker Basket

The sun was shining a little too stridently upon the carriage as it rolled along the streets of the French Quarter. But the young woman tried not to worry—she would simply lose herself in these rare moments of her life. She listened as the horses' hooves made a cadence which befitted her wedding day—she actually wondered how the tapping of hooves could sound so perfect. She began to think that everything was set to her rhythm today, and for that she was grateful.

Her father sat next to her in the open coach, in his rented tuxedo, with one of his gloved hands occasionally holding hers. He seemed to understand how much she needed his steady hand. Her dress—overpriced but basking in Vera Wang's authoritative but silky workmanship—spread out over Calla's thin knees and ankles, brushed against the red velvet of the inner carriage, and at times floated up and down as the wheels fought against the rough pavement. She looked down at the wicker basket, filled with lilies, carnations, and other fine flowers. Her father had given them to her as they boarded the carriage only minutes before. Each flower in the basket was as purely white as her dress. She smiled and regarded her father as someone who deserved to spend these moments with her, as someone who deserved to be in her life again.

Without turning her head too quickly, not wanting to spoil her hair, Calla allowed herself to look upon the passing restaurants and tourist shops. All those faces, out-of-towners for certain, making their way along the famed streets. They seemed to be searching for moments like these, moments that would capture the essence of New Orleans. She instinctively knew that she mustn't rush through everything that would happen; she must wait for the carriage to pull alongside the downstairs to the lobby, hoping to run into a few family members waiting. They were surprised to find that every seat in the lounge was filled with a great-aunt, big mama, cousin, or sibling of William's or Calla's. The oldest of them planted kisses and hugs on William's stiff face and shoulders. Others remained sitting, obviously not wanting to lose their seats; they simply waved a hand or yelled across the lobby. "Any moment, now," someone said, meaning that William should keep watch for the moment when he must post himself outside the hotel and escort Calla in. Everyone had heard about this grand entrance. William assured the waiting guests that the doorman would warn him when the carriage approached the hotel. This said, the crowd settled down again, and sat with their arms crossed, over their purses or just their laps, with their eyes darting furtively around, sure they were in for a beautiful treat when the wedding finally started.

The carriage rolled on, as if it could not stop, and Calla got lost in her deepest worries. She would not have noticed the car that went down the crossing street, had not the wheels gone screeching by. The people on the sidewalk commented about it in their own way—amazed that someone could be so reckless when all these pedestrians were about. Perhaps they had begun to feel protective of this bride and did not want her day to be spoiled.

But Calla noticed few of these things. She didn't see that a number of tourists had collected like schools of fish behind the carriage, all of them wanting to follow the bride to her destination. She didn't see them raising their cameras high in the air, trying to get a picture of the stunning bride. She didn't see how they smiled and felt giddy amongst themselves, and chatted about their luck, so happy to have stumbled upon a wedding in the French Quarter.

Calla was actually becoming annoyed with her father—she couldn't imagine anyone sitting so peacefully and silent when her nerves were fraying. Where were the worry lines on his face, as there must be a thousand or more on hers? Every minute or so, her father squeezed her hand gently. A small reminder that he was there? If only he would truly speak to her. Of all the years of her life, this was the one time when they were completely alone. There had been so many questions that needed answering. Why he had gone away and left Calla and her mother. This seemed traitorous to Calla, for she saw herself as deserving only the best things in life, which included having a full-time father. Although Calla had been seven at the time, she often thought of calling him over the years and telling him how angry she was about her broken family.

There were so many times when she had needed him: like when she fell down the stairs at school and broke her ankle (she was only in fifth grade then); or when she got into fights at school, with the girls who wanted to prove themselves at someone else's expense; or when she sat up many late nights, worried that she would never find a man to love. She had really needed him when she turned twenty-one and thought she knew everything, when she fell for the wrong guy, one who had a way of verbally abusing her and making her feel completely worthless. It seemed too late to call her father then; she had gotten used to him not being there. After that, there was no need to call him and tell him she had figured out the intricacies of life on her own.

She and her father had only reconnected after Calla's mother called to tell him about the wedding. How surprised Calla had been when he wanted to come and escort her down the aisle. She felt a small joy in disappointing him: she and William would walk down the aisle together. After a few months of punishing him, she told her father that he could ride with her in the carriage, from Louis Armstrong Park to the hotel. He quickly let go of his disappointment and said yes, that he would do whatever she asked. The basket of flowers was obviously his attempt to woo Calla back into his life for good.

So why was he not being more attentive to her now, Calla wondered. Clearly, he could see that she was slowly losing her mind, that soon she would grab the train of her dress, leap out of the carriage, and go running the few blocks to the hotel. Then she felt her father's hand squeeze hers. This time, he turned to her, and seeing her strained look, smiled and said, "You are beautiful."

Her heart suddenly remembered how it felt to have a father. All of her seemed to be melting. Perhaps it was only the hot afternoon sun. When she and William had planned the wedding, they forgot to think of the heat—today it was burning her to the core. She could peel a layer of skin off and throw it on the pavement if she wanted to. The horses would trample it, and finally she'd hear a different tone to the horses' hooves echoing against the buildings. What had once sounded so perfect was now working on her nerves. Calla felt her father's hand wrap even tighter around hers. She had nothing left to do but reach over and place her other hand on top of his.

William was also beginning to show signs of nervousness. The guests continued to arrive, each walking in and, upon noting that there were no seats, backing off slightly until they found a pillar or a wall to lean against. The time for Calla's arrival—2:00 p.m.—was still 10 minutes away, and both William and the guests began to question why they were still standing in the lobby. William and Calla had not hired a wedding planner, and had "fallen out," as they say, with the hotel's planner. This left William's best man in charge. He stood proudly, next to William, as if to say, whatever happened, it wouldn't be his fault.

Guillory went to the door, and cursorily peered outside, looking for the carriage. "No sign of them," the doorman assured him. Guillory returned and relayed the message. At this point, those guests who had seats sank their bottoms deeper, and those standing switched from one leg to the other. The ushers came, found the crowd waiting in the lobby, and chastised them for not finding their places in the courtyard. Suddenly, everyone felt stupid and began to trudge their way to the courtyard at the center of the hotel. Onlookers in the adjacent dining areas could hardly be blamed for thinking a herd of elephants or other migrating animals were coming through. But this particular wedding party cared less about what these high-class hotel guests may have thought of them.

The ushers rushed to take the mothers of the bride and groom to their assigned seats. Each of the ladies felt like royalty then, never having been escorted into such a lovely setting. The courtyard bloomed with hydrangeas and giant roses, which had been integrally placed according to the couple's imagination. Large floral trees and ferns made the area look and feel like Adam and Eve's garden; some of the palms reached as high as the third and fourth floors, with the fanned limbs hanging over onto the veranda and blocking the onlooker's view into the hotel rooms. A few hotel guests stood on their balconies, holding a Hurricane or a Creole Bloody Mary loosely in their hands.

They waved down at the wedding party, who waved back and shouted things like "Hello!" and "This is the Chassen wedding" and "Go, William and Calla!" Meanwhile, a three-tiered lighted fountain bubbled nearby, completing the extravagance of the setting. The guests couldn't help but look around in amazement, noticing just how far their cars had brought them from the miserliness of the projects where many of them still lived.

When the hotel was finally in sight, Calla felt as though she could breathe. No more thoughts about jumping from the carriage and running to the hotel, with her veil wafting after her. How long before her father would have come chasing behind? Yes, those thoughts were now gone. She saw the doorman step inside for a moment, and she knew he was calling for William. The carriage driver, too, seemed anxious; he turned and said to Calla and her father, "Just a few moments, folks, and we'll be there."

Calla took this to mean they would stop as soon as the carriage came flush with the heavy front doors of the iconic hotel. This part of the ceremony she and William had not practiced; how difficult could it be for William to walk up to Calla, take her hand, and lead her from the buggy? Calla already knew where she would place her left foot, when it descended first. Then the right, which would barely touch the bottom rung of the step before she fell into William's arms. He would hold her for a few moments, William would say something wonderful in her ear, and she would no longer be nervous or afraid or impatient, for she would have made it to the moment she had been waiting for all day long. From there, she and William would walk the short distance to the courtyard where her family and friends would, upon seeing them, burst into the loudest cheers she could imagine.

"Come quickly," the doorman motioned to William. He had only to say it once. William had been waiting for this moment his entire life—even if it was just now that he realized it. He and Guillory hugged—a proper pat on each other's back—then William started for the door. His legs appeared so long now and the guests imagined he was at least seven feet tall. His strides tackled the distance so quickly, leaving the guests' eyes to remain at the entrance of the courtyard until William

The Persimmon Trail

Until that day, whenever we talked about the path, there was still a level of innocence that bled into our conversations. There were, ever present, our father's true life footprints along the way—caked in mud and hardened by the light of day—and our mother's sad admonitions about every man making honest footprints in the sand. There were the sweet smelling Johnnie Walker whisky bottles that sometimes lined the trail, thrown into a wayward bush for protection against little people like us detecting them. We found the empty bottles anyway, and longed for just a taste of the deceiving nectar. There were also the dueling persimmon trees that lined the path; they seemed to have obstinately sat themselves down in the small valley that separated our property from our neighbor woman's. Oh, the moments we spent cultivating our knowledge of those trees: when to break open one of the fruits and when to leave it lying on the ground. Sometimes even the darkest and softest of the persimmons fooled us, and we were left wrestling with an awkward bitter taste that remained with us long afterward.

On this particular, warm day we were slightly surprised when we saw one of the neighbor woman's several children, a girl named Maia, come running down the path to our house. Before long, she was down the small hill, through the valley of persimmon trees, over the cow fence (so named because it was the only thing that could keep our Holstein Becky from getting out), through the baby oaks that stood staunchly around like they were watching out for such things, then under our yard fence and up the side lawn. She then stood on our porch steps, all bent over and breathing hard like she had, in just those few moments, completed her trial run at the Olympics.

"Where your Daddy?" she asked.

"He in town, getting feed and stuff," one of us said, but all of us were wondering, "What she want with him?"

Maia seemed perplexed for a minute, then asked, "Where your Mama?"

"In the house," we said, snidely—where else would our mama be if we were sitting out on the porch and she wasn't? Wherever our mother went, we would find a way to tag along—she didn't seem to have the heart to make us stay home, even though our sister Nonna was old enough to take care of us.

Anyway, instead of knocking at the door and waiting patiently for our mother to come out, the girl stood there screaming, "Mrs. Claire! Mrs. Claire!" about as loud as she could. Parts of her voice must have gone stumbling back down the trail from where she had come—the rest seemed to float around our yard before it sifted through the front of the house and back into the kitchen, where our mother was trying to prepare us something for lunch, and probably with her mind on whether or not she had anything to cook for supper.

Soon enough, though, our mother was at the screened door, still wiping her hands on her apron. "What is it, child?" she asked.

"It's my Mama, she need Mr. … I mean, she need somebody to come quick."

Now we all knew, and guessed what everyone else this side of the moon knew, that Maia's mother and our mother did not get along; as far as we knew, they didn't even talk to each other. We knew it had something to do with our father and his being out late at night, but no one talked to us kids about such things. We had to gather information as best we could. We just accepted the idea that our mother and Maia's mother were separated by a few fences for more reasons than one.

So, our hearing the girl say her mother wanted our mother to come to her house seemed unreasonable to us; the truth is that even Maia didn't seem happy to have spoken the words out loud. Apparently, us kids weren't alone in thinking this because a candidly sick look shot across our mother's face. It was one of those scowls we sometimes saw on her face when we had done something extra stupid and she wanted to say something but couldn't because if she did, the only thing that would come out of her mouth would make her explode into a zillion pieces.

"Well, what she need?" our mother managed to say; her body was then leaning hard against the door frame.

"She say she having the baby, and she need help," Maia said, dryly, with a gulp to get it all the way out.

"Well now," the rest of us seemed to sigh. The neighbor woman was having her baby. We pictured our mother remaining there against the door frame, doing nothing, and leaving Maia, and her mother, to fend for themselves. We just knew she was about to tell Maia to go find someone else to help her with her troubles. But this didn't happen. Instead of flat-out refusing to do anything, we saw our mother leap quickly into action. Just like that, it was like the world started churning turning before our eyes. Our mother's body went straight and rigid, down to the last hair on her head, it seemed. She wrung her hands in her apron, whether out of habit or a consuming need to calm herself. But swiftly, she was like a commander at sea, pumping all of us into motion, unleashing the sails that were our hearts—like she was making ready for a journey.

Midwives in those days were punctual and knew how to be found if they weren't at home. Perhaps this is why our mother did not stop at the neighbor woman's house, not even to let Maia out of the car to return to her waiting mother and tell her that help was on the way. Our faces smudged against the back windows of our mother's '63 Olds mobile as we went speeding past the woman's house. Our mother hadn't long gotten the used car, and we were still breaking it in with our own little dirty finger marks and spit stains. None of us dared ask why we didn't stop, not even Maia, who sat back in the seat as though she were experiencing her first ride at a carnival. The smile on her face was unmistakable joy, and a greedy one at that.

Mrs. Dorothea was the closest midwife to us. When we pulled into her yard, it was obvious that she was not at home. She and our mother were best friends and we knew, as if by instinct, when she was home and when she was not. Mrs. Dorothea didn't own a car; she didn't even have a carport. Wherever she was gone, it would have to be on "Moe and Joe," as we used to say, meaning her two feet. Our hearts had calmed down but soon again began to billow, understanding that our mother would have to go in search of Mrs. Dorothea, or another midwife. Living so far out in the country like we did, away from the nearest hospital, midwives were specialists and it was necessary to have more than one of them around. Their skill more often came from their experience of successfully bringing children into the world. And everyone knew Mrs. Dorothea was the best; she was certainly the closest at hand and was, we assumed, the one our mother would search for.

But instead of immediately cranking up the car again, our mother surprisingly said, to no one in particular, "Go knock at the door." It was obviously a safe measure; we all understood how ceremonial that knock would be. Perhaps our mother was still hoping Mrs. Dorothea was home, so that she would not have to go farther and look for her.

Our brother, Jack, who was sitting up front with our mother and our older sister, Nonna, jumped from the car and skipped and hopped all the way to the door. Our mother shook her head at this; we could tell she was thinking, "That boy is always playing." Jack's knocking sounded like the woodpecker that lodged in one of the light posts in our front yard—there was no stopping, just continuous knocking until our mother called Jack back to the car.

"What we gonna do now," he asked when he had settled himself in the seat again. Those of us in the back seat looked at Maia and wondered the same thing. She looked like she could be one of us, as she peered out the window, still on her magical ride.

"This time of day, she might be at Edwina's," our mother said. Mrs. Edwina was Mrs. Dorothea's disproportionately unblessed twin sister. The thought of her made our skin twitch. She towered above all other women—and many men—and had a face that had been disfigured—in the war? or in a bar fight with a couple of men?—we didn't know for certain, but we imagined these kinds of things. She looked like a quiet monster had taken possession of her. Our bodies slumped down into the seat for survival's sake, and this was before our mother cranked up the car and headed in Mrs. Edwina's direction.

There were the tales our father had told us about Mrs. Edwina's going on night runs, looking for bad little children to eat. All of it, though outrageous, seemed highly plausible because we had personally seen her eat the strangest of things. Once before, when our mother had for the last time visited Ms. Edwina, the woman had offered us turtle stew that had turned into rattlesnake stew. "I only had the one turtle," she said to my mother, "so I throwed in a rattler to make it stretch. I betcha it ain't easy feeding a big brood like your'n everyday. This here stew'll fill 'em up!"

All of us kids had gone running from her house and stood squirming by the car when our mother finally came out to leave. She was carrying a large bowl of the snake stew in her hands. We knew that in these Louisiana parts, you couldn't turn people down when they offered you food. Only when we arrived home and had sat down in the comfort and safety of our own home did our mother explain that she had politely asked Mrs. Edwina to put the stew in a bowl so that we could share it with our father. This never happened, of course. When our father came home, he threw the stew out the back door, and even the dogs wouldn't eat it. He then suggested, clearly and without question, that we stop hanging out at Mrs. Edwina's house in the first place.

Mrs. Edwina's house was barely a mile farther down the road, just off the highway, so it didn't take us long to get there. The car rolled to a quiet stop just beyond a large pine tree that stood towering over the front of her house. We waited. Soon enough, the large woman came to the door but held herself back, as though she needed to be coaxed from her house. Our mother opened the car door and stood with one leg on the ground and the other in the car, one hand on the steering wheel, leaving her left arm sitting on top of the open door. Our mother's stance seemed to suggest a standoff.

"Afternoon," our mother said.

"Afternoon," Ms. Edwina said, as she allowed a little more of her largeness to come out of the house.

"Looking for Dot," our mother said, not moving any farther from the car.

"Well, you'd do better to look someplace else," Mrs. Edwina said; then she came fully from her house and stood at the very edge of the porch. We could hear the floor boards squeaking from the weight of her. "I ain't seen Dot around here since day 'fore yestidy."

"We kind of desperate," my mother said. "Need to find her."

"What for?" Ms. Edwina asked, as she started moving down the

"Looking for you," our mother said.

"Well, don't let me be caught and sold for groceries! You know, people don't come looking for you for no good reason."

"It's her time," our mother said and pointed her head back to Maia as she spoke. "Her mama's having the baby." Our mother and Mrs. Dorothea understood each other's language, their way of speaking things, so it didn't take long for Mrs. Dorothea to get the gist of it.

"And you looking for me to deliver it?"

"Who else need to do it? I'm already traipsing up and down the highway trying to get help. You know how some people feel about that woman." When our mother said these things, in a lower voice, she placed both hands on the steering wheel, and it was clear that she was speaking solely to her friend. Mrs. Dorothea's head was almost fully inside the car now, and she and our mother were obviously peering inside each other's souls. Our mother's arms then went straight and tight against the wheel. She had that same rigid look that had come on her face when Maia first came looking for her. That look said she didn't have all the answers.

Mrs. Dorothea remained leaning inside the car, but it was obvious she was trying to think of a way out. Her eyes maneuvered around those of us in the car. They settled on Maia and seemed to grow darker and meaner as she stared at the girl. Some of us noticed for the first time the resemblance between Mrs. Dorothea and Mrs. Edwina.

"Get in the car, Dot," our mother finally said.

Mrs. Dorothea moved her arm from the top of the car and began her slow trek around to the other side of the car, mumbling as she walked. Meanwhile, our mother told Jack to jump in the back seat. At this point, the back seat was simply crawling with arms and legs, and one or two of us had to kneel on the floor. Pushing Nonna over next to our mother, Mrs. Dorothea got in and sat with one arm dangling out the open window, with a cigarette between two fingers.

On the way out of the Fields, the gang of boys had obviously seen a car approaching and had prepared themselves with handfuls of china berries. But when they saw it was our mother, they seemed to remember the dusting she had given them earlier and they stood to the side, allowing our car to pass without throwing even one berry. Our mother waved and gave them a pleasing smile as payment. But we kids yelled out the window and laughed and called them every name we could think of. Looking out the back window, we made gestures with our fingers and pulled our ears wide, leaving our tormentors with something to remember us by until the next time.

There was silence in the car then, all of us expecting that our mother and Mrs. Dorothea would start up one of the somewhat cryptic conversations they usually had—our mother grumbling overall about life with our father, and Mrs. Dorothea always telling our mother to leave, to take us kids and go someplace else. Whenever they had these conversations, it was always obvious that Mrs. Dorothea cared deeply for our mother, and that she only said these things because she thought our mother could be happier away from our father. And it was just as obvious that Mrs. Dorothea was wasting her breath. We knew by the way that our mother treated our father—always cooking him the best meals and setting them out for him and making his bath and the way she allowed him to tease her and let him make excuses for coming home so late at night—all that kind of stuff told us that she was sticking around for the day when she believed he would become the husband she needed. She seemed intent on staying put, and Mrs. Dorothea was intent on her "waking up and smelling the stink in the air," as she said.

But the conversation on this day, when we went driving around in search of a midwife to deliver our neighbor woman's child, would enlighten us in ways we hadn't imagined.

"Why didn't you try to find someone else? You know I don't have nothing to do with that heifer." It was Mrs. Dorothea who struck the first note.

"The girl said her mama's having the baby now, Dot."

"What you care, either way?"

"Dot, come on," and our mother once again turned her head slightly and peered back at Maia. She seemed wholly concerned about the girl's feelings getting hurt.

"I don't care who hears it," Mrs. Dorothea said. "I'll tell her mama the same thing. That woman ain't got no right asking you for help with nothing, not even throwing her dirty dishwater out her back door."

"Dot, that's enough." Our mother was getting heated up, and we knew Mrs. Dorothea had better be quiet. But Mrs. Dorothea went on.

"We talking about a man that can't seem to find his way home at night," she said. This was a side of the conversation that we had often heard, but Mrs. Dorothea, it was like she couldn't stop talking. She seemed intent on her truth seeing the light of day.

Our mother said, very slowly, as though she was trying to calm Mrs. Dorothea down, "I can put all that aside for now; we talking about a unborn baby here."

It didn't work. Mrs. Dorothea seemed to get angrier: "You right about that, a baby that's his, no doubt. Might be another one of your children's half brothers or sisters. You hear that Nonna? Jack? Nicki? You know you got another little sister or brother about to come into the world?" Mrs. Dorothea turned around in the seat as though she expected an answer from those of us she had named.

But our mother answered for us. She slammed hard on the brakes and the car jumped and skidded to a stop, literally smashing us into the back of the front seat and into each other. Dust from the roadway caught up with the now stopped car and rolled through the open windows, taking up what little room we had left for breathing. Soon we were coughing and fanning, searching for clean, tasteless air.

"I said that's enough!" We heard our mother literally screaming this. Then, she was looking at Mrs. Dorothea with anger; her eyes were jumping up and down, fast, and almost looked like they would get stuck up in the top of her head sooner than later. Her teeth clenched and she bore down on her friend. Those of us in the back seat thought of a rabid dog and what things might make a human animal go mad.

Mrs. Dorothea planted her eyes straight ahead and brought the hand that held her cigarette to her face. She didn't puff right away; she waited, as though she would say something first, then thought better of it. She pulled in hard on the cigarette smoke and let it settle into her body. We in the back seat thought she might never exhale, but slowly she allowed the smoke to trickle out into a little river that floated out the window and got lost in the remaining dust.

Neither woman said anything else as we rode along. We would be at Maia's house soon, and the girl would finally get out of the car and most likely go running to check on her mother. The rest of us would continue to ask our hearts what had just happened. As it was, we looked around at each other and wondered about the things we were completely sure of, or whether or not we could be sure of anything. How could the neighbor woman's baby be our father's baby, too? And what did Mrs. Dorothea mean when she said we had half brothers and sisters? Some of us wondered if she was crazy. Our siblings were all in the car, there, now, with our mother. This is what we knew, or thought we knew. We continued to think on these things as we pulled in front of Maia's house. The girl crawled over several laps, making her way out of the car. She then ran into the house, as though she were escaping from us.

Mrs. Dorothea took one more look at our mother. She moved her mouth to speak, to perhaps say, "I'm sorry," but no words came.

"Hurry," our mother said, as though she were pushing Mrs. Dorothea out of the car with her last bit of will and determination.

We all sat watching as Mrs. Dorothea finally walked up the steps of the little shack of a house. It was easy to see why our mother could spare pity for the neighbor woman. All those kids in that little rundown house. We didn't have much, but they had even less than us. We began to see how she might think our mother should share our father. Or maybe she thought her only option in life was to take what she needed. We wondered about this as the door closed behind Mrs. Dorothea—the midwife who was late and obstinate, and who wished that she had not been found.

The youngest of us, Nicki, Will, Karen, and Yvette asked our mother if we could take the path back to the house to gather persimmons. She nodded her head without speaking. Jack and Nonna, remained in the car, out of support for our mother, or perhaps because the persimmon trail now seemed a little tainted.

We jumped from the car and went running off toward our house—we went in the name of looking for sweet, juicy persimmons, but what we really wanted to do was race our mother home. We zipped down through the trees and under the fences and over obstacles in our path. We threw off our shoes when we reached the wide yard, choosing to feel the cool grass between our toes as we ran.

Our mother had already parked the car and was walking up the porch steps, with Jack and Nonna trailing behind her, like baby chicks still learning how to survive in life. Those of us who had sought to race our mother home came sidling up to the porch and didn't seem to care that she was the winner in this race of our making. In our hearts, we wanted her to win.

surely have given us away.

Miss Rose and Miss Emma, probably upon hearing the gravelly approach of a vehicle, came from their house—a side door, off from the kitchen. Their faces turned almost giddy when they saw our mother stepping her bountiful self out of the driver's seat. All of us children, including our oldest sister who sat up front with our mother, knew not to move an inch from the vehicle. We sat like butterflies, our wings flexing softly, wistfully sunning ourselves in the afternoon sun—I am sure we had that appearance, that we were changing or molting into greater beings just happy to be in these women's presence.

"Well, hello, Claire," Miss Rose might say, as she switched her dress tail out of her way as she walked. Somehow she was taller in these moments, unencumbered by nature's bending of her back and the slowness of her stride.

"We weren't expecting you today," Miss Emma would add, looking over to Miss Rose for confirmation. Miss Emma was the younger of the two, and understandably her smile was the brightest, although her speech less perspicacious.

"No, Ma'am," our mother would agree. "We was just out and about and thought we'd stop by and see how y'all was doing." This was an outright lie, or at least one of those little lies one tells to keep faith with others. The truth is that our mother generally planned these occasions, in a way—like the times when she and our father were fighting and she needed to get away, or when the bills were so heavy she didn't think we'd be able to survive. Some of the visits happened mysteriously when we, ourselves, had little food at home. I guess, to our mother, these seemingly unexpected visits were actually lifelines to her sanity.

"Well, Claire," Miss Rose would say, "that's just like you to check up on us." This was said in a tone that suggested the requisite part of the conversation was over.

From there, Miss Rose would mosey over to the outside lunch table and offer our mother one of the four seats that hovered around the table. One side of the table sat beneath a crepe myrtle tree bursting with blooms, so that Miss Rose ceremoniously stepped upon a carpet of the rich purple color on the way to her seat. Miss Emma did not sit across from our mother, not immediately.

"Thank you, Miss Rose," our mother would graciously say before she pulled out one of the remaining wrought iron chairs. These chairs looked as though they had been drenched and re-drenched in white paint over the many years of the women's lives.

Miss Rose would ask our mother if she'd already had lunch.

Our mother had come to realize that it was a rhetorical question, for no matter what time of day it was that we visited, Miss Emma would immediately begin to prepare the afternoon meal that she would serve to us. It did not matter what our mother's answer was, yes or no, it was understood by all present that we would take part in this lunching ritual.

While Miss Emma was in the kitchen preparing the sandwiches, our mother and Miss Rose spoke softly among themselves, not because they were trying to hide their conversation, but because they were speaking of things that they assumed we, on the back of the truck, could not understand—it was just better that we did not hear any of it. But what we noticed was the effort Miss Rose was making to befriend our mother. Their conversations became that of friends.

Every so often we might hear our mother's voice rise into a surprising "Oh!" and we knew Miss Rose had said something that was too incredulous for our mother to believe. Later that night, when we were home again and had partaken of our meager supper, we children would hear our mother speak of many of those things—to our father—that she and Miss Rose had so quietly discussed. Sometimes we would have to wait until one of our mother's friends visited our house, or until we went to visit her best friend Mrs. Dorothea's house, before we could overhear these things: gossip mostly about people in our community who weren't getting along in life so well, or more serious topics like the fact that the schools would soon be desegregated and we colored kids would be bussed to a different school.

Soon enough, Miss Emma would reappear at the kitchen door, peering out so that her cheek was freckled against the screen. She'd gently call to her sister, "Rose, dear," and Miss Rose would turn away from our mother and attempt to quickly gather her self up from the chair so that she could assist Miss Emma.

"Y'all need some help?" our mother would call out, to Miss Rose's back, which was now humped over from the sitting spell, so that even in rushing, Miss Rose only moved slowly to the door.

Miss Rose would get close enough to the house that she felt she could ignore our mother's question; she allowed her facial expression to say she had not heard our mother. She'd open the door carefully, for Miss Emma stood on the other side holding a tray with sandwiches and a couple glasses of sweet tea.

"Careful," Miss Emma would say, just to be sure.

Miss Rose would manage to wrestle the tray from her sister without spilling the sweet tea onto the sandwiches. She'd then begin her slow trek back to the table, where our mother now stood with her arms out, ready to leap for the tray if Miss Rose fell or simply lost her strength and couldn't carry the tray any further. Miss Rose would labor with the tray, her face leaning so close to the glasses of tea that she could sip a little from each glass if she so chose. Meanwhile, Miss Emma would have gone back into the kitchen and come forth with another tray, this one filled with the remaining glasses of tea. On the next round, she would return with a bowl of corn chips or potato chips and small paper plates and napkins. When both ladies returned to the table, they would look to our mother, for it was now her turn to act in this small drama, by bringing us children into their midst.

The task was never difficult. Our mother would barely turn her head toward us before we had leapt from the sides of the truck like bunnies from a burning bush. We quickly lined up single-file behind our mother. The oldest child of us came last, as if planned, so that she could go about keeping order and silence as the meal was being given to us.

Generally, the sandwiches that Miss Emma prepared were pressed ham with cucumbers and mayonnaise on white bread, or home-cooked turkey slices with a special sauce that Miss Emma made, but occasionally when we arrived at the table we would find that Miss Emma had chosen to feed us pimento cheese sandwiches instead. We did not like pimento cheese, at all, except for one or two of the oldest of us—even though Miss Emma usually served her homemade brand, with fresh cheese, mayonnaise, and sweet peppers. She even trimmed the crusts and cut the sandwiches and sometimes served them with watercress. Fortunately, these occasions were rare (perhaps Miss Emma realized it was more trouble than it was worth).

And even though we couldn't appreciate it, no matter how many times Miss Emma served us pimento cheese, we nevertheless ate the food and always looked forward to the times when our mother visited with these old ladies.

As the years passed, we noticed that Miss Emma was preparing pimento cheese sandwiches on all our visits, and what was worse, this was store-bought pimento cheese. And even though we hated those sandwiches, we would eat them (after all, it was food, and more often than not, we were hungry and would eat whatever we were given). There was something about the orangey gooeyness of the sandwiches that reminded most of us of the mixed up pieces of crayons we often had to use at school. This color seemed all used up, and tended to remind us that we were second class citizens. We just couldn't get comfortable with it.

One day, things changed forever. Miss Rose's death angel had come, our mother told us. Miss Emma actually called our mother and gave her the sad news. Our mother shed open tears in front of us.

"You will come?" Miss Emma asked her, speaking of Miss Rose's funeral. Our father said Miss Emma obviously didn't understand the social walls that our mother would have to pass through in order to go to Miss Rose's funeral. It was known that a lot of their family members didn't care for us colored.

"Yes, ma'am, Miss Emma," our mother said. "If you think it's all right."

On the day of the funeral, our mother gathered us, her small brood, all of us dressed in clothes we only wore on special occasions—the girls in various chiffon dresses, resembling flowers unsullied and plucked from the garden; the boys in black pants, with their Sunday white, short-sleeved shirts buttoned to the neck, and all of us with our good shoes on.

Walking into the funeral parlor was the first test of our mother's nerves, and more than once she seemed to be questioning her choice of being there. But her duty came calling, and she would remain there grieving with these people, most of them not wanting her there. We walked bravely in and commissioned an entire bench near the back of the small parlor. Family members of Miss Rose's did not turn their heads back to the front until we had situated ourselves and sat staring back at them. Then, as if the matter was settled, small conversations struck back up, and eyes no longer rolled back to us. Instead they focused upon the white and pink casket that held Miss Rose's dead body.

After a prayer had been said and Ecclesiastes had been read, and many of us children had pondered on the truths of there being "a time for everything," a minister stood and asked if anyone would come and speak a few words in Miss Rose's honor. There was only one family member, other than Miss Emma, who seemed interested—a brother who lived a few parishes over—and his departing words to his sister were terse and formal, almost as though someone had paid him to speak.

Miss Emma waited until it was clear that no one else would stand. She climbed to her feet, standing wearily, but she seemed "bound and determined," as we always said, to say just how much Miss Rose had meant in her life. But no words came; she stood there weeping, as though she might soon give in to death as well. No one moved to help her; they didn't understand what was happening. Our mother knew, and we knew: Miss Emma had in that moment realized she was alone in the world. Perhaps all of Miss Emma's future passed through her mind as she stood there, breaking down from the weight of it all.

But even us children were stunned when our mother stood up and began to speak. "I've known Miss Rose for 'bout ten years now. We'd just moved here from the city." We children stood up, flanking her on both sides, as if we understood and must therefore be accomplices to our mother's sense of obligation. She continued: "She saw me down at the grocery store, trying to make my few dollars stretch."

Miss Emma sat down softly on the bench, obviously comforted by our mother's words.

"My children," our mother said, "was looking kinda thin I guess, and Miss Rose asked me where we lived. I told her down near the creek, in that little house just off from the highway. She said she knew where it was, and then she just kept on doing her shopping. I figured she had forgot about us 'cause I didn't see her in the store no more. Well, I fiddled around getting a little flour and oil and this and that. I was outside getting the groceries and the children in the car (we had that Oldsmobile then), and Miss Rose came up to me and said she wanted us to come visit her. 'Can't miss it,' she said, 'it's the only house over on William's Road. It's got camellia bushes along the driveway.' I told her 'Yes, ma'am,' and put it in the back of my mind. I figured she was just being nice and all, but something kept telling me to listen up, that she might'a meant it."

By now, all the heads in the funeral parlor had turned and the people sat listening contentedly to our mother. A few even nodded their heads as they heard our mother talk about Miss Rose. Miss Emma, most of all, was enjoying the story, for she had no doubt heard Miss Rose's version, on many of the evenings she and Miss Rose had sat around a quiet fire, or at the kitchen table, and they repeated the stories that represented their lives. Tears began to well up again in Miss Emma's eyes, but she lifted her head proudly, as though she would, with gravity's help, force the tears back somehow.

"Not much longer," our mother continued, "I'd say about a month, we was on our way to town and just about the time we was about to pass Miss Rose's house, the truck slowed up, like we was running out of gas or something. But it wasn't that; I looked at the needle and the truck had gas. I always said after that day that it was the Lord who made us stop. We pulled into the yard, like the truck had a mind of its own. All them beautiful flowers was the first thing welcomed us. The children pulled off some of the bushes as we drove in, thinking I didn't see 'em, but I did. Miss Rose didn't care none either. She'd come out when she heard us drive up. 'Get out, stay a while,' she said, like she'd been friends with us for years.

"That was the first time we stopped and had lunch with Miss Rose and Miss Emma, but not nearly the last. It got so, some months when the children was out of school, and I was having trouble feeding 'em all, we'd stop by and visit Miss Rose and Ms. Emma way more than a few times a month. No matter how often we come, her and Miss Emma always treated us good. They wouldn't let us get away from there without eating something. It got so the children looked forward to the visits as much as I did, 'even if it's pimento cheese,' they used to say. It's a acquired taste, I told them."

Heads nodded in agreement, as if everyone had dined on those pimento cheese sandwiches at one time or another.

"Well, that's all I wanted to say." Our mother was beginning to close her little speech. "Just that Miss Rose was a wonderful friend to me and my children, and Lord knows we're going to miss her." And with this last statement, our mother fell back hard in her seat, and she allowed the tears that wanted to fall to drop gracefully upon her lap.

We gathered closer around her because we, unlike anyone else in the room it seemed, had felt nature's pity and truly knew how lucky we had been to know Miss Rose. Perhaps it was the sight of our mother's vulnerability in those moments of sorrow, or perhaps it was our own sadness over the loss.

As the years passed and we spoke of Miss Rose and those many afternoons spent at her house, the one thing we would remember clearly was the looks on our faces when we first uncovered the napkin from our plates and saw those pimento cheese sandwiches. The older we got, all of us grew to love the Southern treat, often eating our mother's version. We found that our mother was right after all; it was an acquired taste.

Doll

She sure was pretty, walking down the cobblestoned, oak-lined lane. The men in the adjoining fields would stand and stretch their long limbs as their raw, cotton-picking fingers pointed to the sky. They'd watch her move slowly down the way. Day after day, the men stood like this—at attention, like stilled flags, symbols of devotion to her. As they stood, watching her, the afternoon sun sent sweat lisping in inches down their backsides. Every slender-footed step she made pulled them closer and closer to her world.

She was a teacher, one of the ones brought down from North Louisiana and nearby states during the early 1900s and housed at an old plantation home in the Florida Parishes. There were others like her but none of them quite as attractive. None of them could affect those hard-working field hands like she did. Each afternoon, after she finished her teaching duties, she alone volunteered (or perhaps it was her appointed errand) to walk the eighth of a mile down the long lane that stretched from the main road up to the steps of the grand house. She would gather the mail from the rusty mailbox and walk slowly back, pretending not to rummage through the letters searching for one with her name on it. And pretending not to notice that all the cotton picking had stopped temporarily, suspended because the men's eyes were upon her.

One day, late in summer and at the top of the afternoon hour, Jill's Son (who was called this because his given name was too hard for most of the regular folk to pronounce) stared so hard at Doll walking down the lane that he suddenly lost all reasonable sense—that part of a conscience that tells a person when not to act foolish—and went tearing off through the cotton field after her. His path would intercept hers just as she reached the mailbox. Most of the men had no clue as to what would come about when this happened, but they did figure, and rightly so, that little good could come from this meeting.

Dust rose from beneath cotton bushes that had already been picked, the men's scouring hands having depleted every bush of its puffs of dirty cotton. The limbs were all but dead; many of them broke and went caterwauling as Jill's Son trampled the field. The dust became a trail that the others used to track his progress. Soon he would come to a complete stop and the dust would drift away.

Doll, herself, noticed and heard him, and when he finally arrived and stood before her, he glistened in a layer of sweat and dirt.

"Good afternoon," she said, as she reached for the mail in the box.

"Afternoon, ma'am," Jill's Son said. They both then stood around, silently holding on to each other's presence.

Meanwhile, back up through the cotton field, the men waited. They were already flabbergasted that Jill's Son had made this move. So they nearly fell to their knees in thanksgiving when they saw Doll and Jill's Son walking together back up the lane, their bodies close, as though this meeting was natural and not made up on the spur of the moment, like it really was. The men's only wish was to know what the man and woman were talking about.

Actually, they weren't talking at all. Doll had turned to go back to the big house, and Jill's Son simply accompanied her. As they moved along, her block heels hit the pavement and resounded against the surrounding oak trees. His feet were bare so he made no sound, although he did wonder if she could hear the thoughts fighting in his head, or the sound of his heart pinging in his chest. He noticed the slow rhythm her small steps made. She wasn't to be hurried; he had often wondered if she moved so slowly down the lane because she knew he and the fellas were watching. Now he knew it was her natural gait. Something else, he thought, to admire about her.

As Jill's Son was taking account of every little thing in Doll's movements, she was wondering how this little scene might end. Would he go all the way with her, and when they reached the long wide steps, would he continue to follow her, even into the house? And would he wish to sit with her and the other four teachers who were living there during the school term? She had to admit that the thought of the young man—dirty and dripping with sweat, his feet caked in the residue of the dark color of the earth—possibly sitting with the others in the big house, was titillatingly sweet. She said nothing; she was suddenly satisfied in his presence.

They would arrive at the steps soon, and the men in the cotton field had yet to take their eyes off Doll and Jill's Son. Somehow they knew they would need to recall every single moment for later. Many of them could not contain their disappointment: soon they would have to get back to work proper, instead of pretending to pull the cotton from its pods, while leaving their eyes to follow Doll and Jill's Son. The men were secretly wondering how Jill's Son would make a further fool of himself. But he just strummed along, walking next to Doll like he and she had been friends forever.

Jill's Son wanted to make a move, even if people would later say, "Yep, that was the moment when he made a complete fool of himself." But what could he do? Ask her name proper?—it was the cotton pickers who had named her Doll, because, from where they stood in the fields, she looked so dainty and breakable. Could he dare speak to her, about her life and why she was in this place, possibly quite far away from home? What was it like being a teacher? What were her dreams… ? No, he couldn't ask any of these things. He would best serve himself if he turned and walked back to the fields and finished stuffing cotton in his sack before the boss man returned. But what could he do if his heart wouldn't allow him to leave her side?

The first of Doll's tiny feet was about to step up the staircase.

"See me," he said, hurriedly.

She turned to him and asked, "What did you say?"

Not sure if he should repeat the outburst, he stumbled back, then quickly recovered his courage. "See me, I said."

"Well," Doll said. "Is that even possible?" The truth is that she had begun to think such a thing was indeed possible. In a flash, she could see herself lying in this beautiful man's arms, late some night, even if beneath the stars, alone with no shelter to cover them. His ruddiness had claimed her heart in just those brief moments. His embarrassment was the first to disappear, and she saw at once how the dirt and wetness on his skin could wash away as well, and how his impressive feet might carry her to their lovemaking bed. All of the outer encumbrances fell away, even the small voice telling her that they could never share a world so intimately.

"Meet me tonight, by the large oak just down there," he said, pointing to one of those great trees that had gotten so old its limbs reached down and buried themselves in the earth. "Do it," he said, "and I'll show you what's possible."

Doll let her foot settle on the step and the other followed. Up and up she went until she disappeared behind the white lace curtains blowing off the gallery. When she allowed herself to look back at him, she was no longer afraid she'd turn into the proverbial block of salt, or whatever happens to a woman who goes courting such trouble. The young man had moved away and was briskly taking himself back to work. The afternoon sun shone hard upon his back.

The seasons changed. Cotton picking turned to sweet potato digging. Doll was now bigger around the belly. She rarely walked the distance to the mailbox but instead went half way, then waited as one of the new male teachers finished the trek and retrieved the mail for her. The cotton pickers were now pulling sweet potatoes from the ground and were not as interested in Doll's movements. The truth is they felt cheated by her, disappointed in the outcome of her and Jill's Son's brief affair. Barely had their tongues gone to wagging when Doll sent Jill's Son away, claiming he could never understand a woman's true desires. The men scoffed at this when Jill's Son, tearfully, repeated it as the end of the cotton season came around. "What do she mean?" they asked. "You don't know how to please a woman, boy?"

Jill's Son assured them this was not true. He even claimed that he had gotten her pregnant, and indeed, they had seen what looked like a small acorn of a bump growing beneath her long, flowing dress. But what would happen to her?, they all wondered. Teachers were meant to be unsullied and virtuous; many had foregone the possibility of having a baby out of wedlock by marrying early, or never placing themselves in the presence of eligible, or desirable men. It seemed that Doll had not been careful enough. No one doubted that she and Jill's Son were sneaking out late at night and being tender with each other beneath the old oak tree. So, why had she sent him away?

That truth would have to come to them piecemeal; Doll would never tell them and Jill's Son was too confused and overturned by love to know what had happened. This was why everyone was shocked to learn that the new male teacher who accompanied Doll down the lane to collect the mail was actually her new husband. Rumor started to circulate that yes, she was pregnant but that this not-so-handsome and slightly older teacher was the father. They had been dating, supposedly, for many years and had finally decided to have a baby and get married, and not necessarily in that order. As word got around, the field hands thought to protect Jill's Son from the news. They spoke about Doll's great pretense almost religiously and without compunction, except when Jill's Son was around, when the men grew quiet and tried to move the conversation around to themselves.

Jill's Son found out the whole truth in the way they most hoped he wouldn't: Doll told him. The men knew, or figured at least, that her version would be too long and too filled with niceties meant to save his drowning heart, but which would do just the opposite and send him into a tailspin of self-hatred.

It happened like this: one day Doll attempted to walk to the mailbox alone—no one at first understood why and figured her new husband was busy preparing for his classes, or she had simply slipped out knowing that Jill's Son would come to her, allowing her to explain herself. He had been down on his knees when she appeared, her small but growing frame ambling down the lane. "Look," some fool said, making Jill's Son aware of her. Actually, none of the men begrudged him this, for at this point they wanted him to find a measure of peace.

Jill's Son sprang to his feet, like water from the earth, and ran at breakneck speed, even faster than the men had remembered when he first went chasing after Doll many months before. He arrived there long before she reached the mailbox, which meant they would have time to talk before she turned and walked back to the mansion.

"Is it true?" he asked, and hoped he wouldn't have to explain what he meant. He did not want to repeat all he had learned while listening in on so many conversations, and how he had found the simple truth that she had been hiding from him.

"Yes," she said. She stopped and pulled him to the side of the cobblestoned path, hoping they would be out of sight from the big house and the men in the field as well.

"Why?" he asked. It was what any man would ask when he found out the woman he loved was married to someone else.

"It's best, Quai," she said. She had begun calling him a shortened version of his given name, Jaliquaious, on those many nights when she lay in his arms. She went on: "I'm sorry. I know words don't mean anything to you, at least not these words." It was true, he had said so many times that the silence between them was worth more than gold. He had grown to treasure it. She wondered if silence could heal what she had done.

"I wish you were dead," he said, "at least then I wouldn't have to watch you prancing around the place with that man."

She couldn't answer.

"Say something," he said. "Anything. I don't want the silence anymore. Just tell me why."

"He's a good man, Quai."

"So am I."

"I know, but..."

"What?"

"We knew it couldn't last, right? You said so yourself. There is no way for us."

"It's... my baby?"

"I promise, this baby will be happy and will have a good life. He will have choices, Quai."

The men in the fields couldn't see the lump, growing thicker inside Jill's Son's throat, or the awful wetness covering his face. He hadn't planned on crying, but he seemed to understand that there are times in a man's life when he can do nothing else. Even with the men watching, and her new husband possibly watching as well, Jill's Son reached for her and drew her to him. She stayed locked in the embrace and took the brunt of the pain that came from his gut.

"Go back," she finally said. The reality of their being there, so out in the open, was too much to ignore. He did as she said, but while turning to go, he caught a look of shame on her face. It was clear and unmistakable. Somehow, this would have to hold him, to stave off the hurt he was feeling. He carried this sign of her weakness back with him through the field, so that when he reached the men again, he was able to fall down on his knees and continue pulling the strings of potatoes from the ground.

Trio

A child in the womb says, "I want to be born so I can know happiness, and when I die, I want to go to heaven so I can see Jesus and walk with the angels. But while I am living, let me find forgiveness no matter the wrongs I've done."

1. Mother's Choice

This begins oddly enough with a modern woman who has two children: one, a fourteen-year-old son who seems destined to play in the NFL, and the other, a girl who is artistic and creative and who looks much older than her twelve years. The mother decides that she only has enough love and attention for one of her children, so she chooses to devote most of her effort to the son, stating to herself, "He will more likely bring peace and good fortune to my life." So, she sends the son to live with his father, who she knows will discipline the son and teach him how to be a proper man. The girl, she keeps with her. She then goes about all but disregarding the girl, as though the girl is barely visible in the mother's life.

The mother has needs—she must have a man in her life, so that even though she is now divorced, she is looking to marry again. The trail of men who come through in the meantime are not marriageable: they lack jobs, cars, and are mostly penniless. They show as much physical interest in the young daughter as they do in the mother. Finally, the mother finds a good candidate, a man who is employed as a clerk at a local Rouses store and who claims that he is steadfastly in love with her. He has a kind face and a stubby belly. Although he, like her, is in his mid-thirties, he is going bald, which makes him feel self-conscious. She can tell that he thinks she is the better catch, and she is okay with that. Barely a week after they have married, the wife awakens to find her husband gone from her side. She listens and cannot hear him stirring about the house. Something tells her to get up and look for him, to bring him back to their marriage bed, but she does not listen to that voice. Since she generally disregards the daughter, it never crosses the mother's mind that her husband has gone looking for that younger touch.

Meanwhile, the new husband has found his way into the daughter's room. He stands over the bed and watches the girl breathe in and out the pure elixir of life, until he cannot contain himself any longer. He tugs at his dirty shorts—he has worn them for three days straight and they are smelly with his lack of freshness. He is completely naked now. Slowly, he maneuvers himself, first one leg and then the other, into the bed, and along comes his body, his arms, then his fatty head. He is attempting to be as quiet and as stealthy as possible. He does not want the girl to wake up, at least not until he is firmly in control of her movements.

When the girl first senses that someone else is in her bed, she imagines that she is dreaming. She has not known her made-up people for a long while—at least not since she has become a young woman—for her mother has told her, now that she has seen the blood between her legs, she has to grow up and put away all her little girl ways. For a brief moment, she thinks her old friends have returned, uninvited yet welcome. But there is something rude and crude about this presence in her bed. It causes her to open her eyes, seeking the true identity of the intruder. It is dark, so dark. Her mother has not allowed her a night light since she was a young girl. Quickly she clears the nightness from her vision; she understands fully who is with her. In that same moment, she feels his arm slide beneath her head and his hand clamp around her mouth. His large, pouty fingers cover much of her face, which means she cannot fully see him. She knows him, though. She would like to say, "Lambert, get away from me; get out of my bed!" She would like to scream and make enormous sounds, not like the small muffles that are coming from her. She briefly thinks, "Where is mother at a time like this?"

Lambert continues what he feels is a smooth assault upon the girl. Now that he has covered her mouth, he can use his other hand to rifle through her loosely fitting nightgown. He is at her stomach, pulling the gown up with his fingers. He goes lower; he is on the precipice of what he likes to call "the female heaven." A small chuckle of joy escapes, too soon. There is something about the laugh, the contempt he obviously feels for her. He knows he has made a mistake, but too late.

The girl buckles abruptly, violently. She bites down hard on the finger that sits in her mouth like a just-cooked sausage—it is wet with her spit at first. Her bite leaves it covered in blood, like the finger sausage has burst open and is easily spewing its juices. When the girl unclamps and lets go, Lambert jerks his hand and his arm away from her. He is lying there on his back now, one hand holding the other up like it needs elevation to survive. The girl takes the moment to release herself from the bed. She does not leave the room, to perhaps run and tell her mother. Instinct tells her that the mother will neither believe her, nor is she likely to care so much. The girl stands by the door, which she has opened. One finger points outward—it is her admonition to him, her warning, her instruction to get out of her room, now.

Lambert is dumbstruck by his luck. He has been eyeing the girl since he first began to date the mother. His entire life he has enjoyed the smells and enchanting obviousness of girls, qualities few women possess. It is something about their innocence that he craves. So, when his new wife's daughter orders him from her room, he finds himself obeying. He now understands that the girl lacks the raw power of weakness, which leaves him utterly cold and limp. Outside the girl's room, he lingers, his body and mind unsure of where to go. Like a stairway leading to his future, he sees a light coming from his new wife's bedroom—the place he also lays his head in slumber. He cannot go there, though. Instead, he walks into the kitchen, then out the back door of the small house. He stands on a makeshift porch, begun by some former boyfriend of his wife's and never finished. Gingerly, he steps on one lonely board after another, until he is at the edge of the structure. The trees surround him and in the darkness he imagines that they are people: his beloved mother, his long dead father, his siblings who never cared so much for him. They stare at him and help him understand; tonight he is seeing the truth of what he is. He has been put out of a girl's room; he, the man. He, the enforcer. This realization frightens him and leaves him feeling empty inside. After some time, he turns to go inside but forgets there are missing boards on the unfinished porch. He does not feel anything after his head is sliced open landing against the sharp corner of post.

Inside, the girl is finishing composing herself, setting her body right again, getting Lambert's junky smell off her. She would like to go to the kitchen and get a drink of water, or better yet, a soft drink that had mysteriously been left for her earlier that evening. She realizes this was Lambert's doing, and she is not so thirsty any more. She climbs back in bed. She does not hear the thud of the man's body as it expires this life.

The next day and the many days which follow are pleasant for the girl but much too awkward for the mother. On Lambert's funeral day, the girl is angry with her mother for being forced to attend the service and she tells her mother that Lambert had come into her room on the night that he died. The mother turns her worn shoulder to her daughter, in disgust? hatred? The mother attends the funeral alone. At some point, the daughter gets used to the mother's disregard of her. She learns to live through the pain of it—of being discounted like she is not valuable. She is a commodity on sale. The daughter finds strength in relying on herself. She struggles no longer. She blossoms as she ages, so that by the time she matriculates into college, she is fully woman and capable of leaving her mother's house for good. The daughter makes good on every promise to herself: she finds a loving husband and he supports her as a budding artist. Her paintings sell well, and she seems destined to be legendary one day.

The mother does not marry again; she finds that she has been bruised by her daughter's accusations; in her heart, she understands the girl has spoken the truth. She begins to wear chagrin like it is her flower. No man seems to want to come within twenty feet of her. She realizes that her attraction is gone, though she cannot explain when or how it happened. She often asks herself if she made the right choice: the boy, who has gone to live with his father, is not living up to his potential. He seems underwhelmed by life and wants little more than to work as a shipping clerk at the local lumber yard. He never makes it to the NFL, nor does he finish college. So the mother's life goes on, often difficult because she has to struggle, especially as she grows older. When the mother reaches the age of fewer and fewer memories, when she is entirely dependent on other souls for her health and for providing and cooking her daily bread, she reaches out to both children. The son tells her he is penniless and can barely care for his own needs. The mother then contacts the daughter, who is rich by the mother's standards. She makes an appeal to the daughter's sense of gratefulness: "If it weren't for me, you'd have nothing." The mother says, "I gave you life." The daughter comes and takes her mother's few things from the closet of the hospital room. She painstakingly helps her mother get dressed. The daughter sees that the clothes are old and extremely well-worn. She makes a mental note that she will have to purchase a new wardrobe for her mother. She will also have to take her for a dental visit; her mother's teeth have mostly rotted away and she needs dentures. The daughter pictures her mother in the spare bedroom, on the first floor, near the downstairs bathroom. She will have to change the sheets and freshen the room before her mother can make the room her own. All sorts of plans enter the daughter's mind. Questions, even. Does she still crave okra and tomatoes, that Louisiana favorite? The daughter knows she will have to speak to her mother's doctor first, and the dietician. As the daughter makes all these mental plans, the mother is being wheelchaired out of the hospital. The daughter walks behind the orderly, which means she does not see the heavy tears that cascade down the mother's face.

Years later, when the mother is finally succumbing to the recompense of old age, she lies on her death bed and asks her daughter to draw nearer.

"Why did you do it?' the mother asks.

"Do what?" the daughter says, even though she knows what her mother is asking.

"Why did you come for me?" the mother asks feebly, her strength failing so quickly. "Because you are my mother," the daughter says, satisfied that she has gotten her one point across in this life. From her days as a young girl, when the only people she could talk to were her imaginary friends, to the days of living in fear that one of her mother's boyfriends would take away her private strength, and even through finding out that she was stronger than they and that she would always fight to survive, even if she had to fight her own mother—all of this comes back to her and bathes her in a voluminous peace that she shares with her mother. There is little more to say, the daughter thinks. She knows her mother has heard her.

Indeed. The mother closes her eyes for goodness this last time. In the arms of her daughter.

2. Falling

Mae and Marshal had been lost in downtown Genoa, Italy for most of the morning when Mae began to understand how she had carelessly given over control of her life to the madman behind the wheel. She had always liked the pretty boys, as Marshal was. He drove, throwing obscenities out his window like still-burning cigarette butts, some flying through the open windows of other motorists and setting them on verbal fire, some flickering off the aged and magnificent buildings and striking innocent pedestrians and perplexed tourists, who had been sitting gently at curbside cafés devouring cups of Italian coffee. When it became impossible for Mae not to speak, she turned towards her husband, with her back resting firmly against the door of the car.

"That must be the hundredth time we crossed that street Vico della Neve." She didn't shout it. The words just fell out of her mouth in a slow even tone, as though they were attempting to make a tentative escape. Marshal was already riled up enough; she didn't want to upset him further.

His body turned slightly toward her, and she flinched. His anger hit her like it always hit her during their marriage: in short, powerful jabs. He didn't touch her, but she felt his will vibrate across the armrest and slap her into a submissive silence.

This wasn't the trip she had planned; she realized this now, bitterly. She was the one who had wanted to see Europe since she was a girl, not him. Yet there he was, as usual, soaking her plans into his. "Let's head up to Marseilles on my days off," he had suggested, out of the blue. It seemed like a good idea until she found out the reason he wanted to go on a trip with her: Dizzy, one of his Navy friends, would be in Marseilles for the week, and he invited them to come up and spend a few days at his hotel. Still she objected: "I don't know who this guy is. Why can't we just go to Venice like I've wanted?"

"Because you ought to want to do what I want to do, okay. Now stop being a bitch about it, and get packed, okay." That was Marshal's answer, final and clear. So she did the thing she always did: she acquiesced, letting him have his way, as she prayed that the trip would turn out to be fun.

They borrowed another friend's car, an '85 VW, which had reached its maturity and had all the appearances of a Rent-a-Wreck. The exterior hadn't begun to rust, yet—probably because that was the only part of the car that was ever cleaned. There was a film of dirt that had become permanently baked to the windshield; the glove compartment was broken and hung down slightly, so that the passenger's legs were never quite comfortable. The true lemon nature of the car: the air conditioner would only function if the temperature outside dropped below 50. This was one of the warmest Julys in Europe's history, and only a noxious heat from the engine came through the vents.

The morning was almost gone and they were still lost in Genoa. The car gave off a sticky wetness that reminded Mae of steamy summers back in Louisiana. I can't be homesick, she thought to herself. Marshal had just gotten stationed at Naples; they would be in Europe for another two years. Thinking of Marshal now, she wriggled and turned her firm body around in the seat. She wondered if she would ever find a relaxed, easy position in that car, with him. All kinds of voices were telling her that she should have just stayed home.

Minutes passed, maybe an hour—Mae was losing her tenuous grasp of time. And without realizing that she had said it: "My Lord, not that same piazza again!"

"Shut up, Mae! If you're not gonna help, just shut up, okay." He had spoken. The heat in the car combined with the act of his driving so uncontrollably caused little sweat balls to form on the outer curls of Marshal's unusually small ears. The back of his mud-brown neck was wet and clung to his knit shirt. He brought the car to a stop, double-parking on a busy one-way street. But instead of chastising Mae, as she thought he would, he leaned the top half of his body out of the car window and began shouting to a peculiar old man standing with his back against a marbled building.

"Hey, que pasa, old man. Look here, I'm looking for the highway… ah shit, what do you call it? You know, the… the freeway." He turned and shrugged his shoulders at Mae, but she didn't know either. She suggested "the autobahn?"

"Yeah, that's it! Where is the autobahn?" fully mouthing the last word.

The Italian nudged himself away from the shadow of the building and said, "Non capisco." He shrugged his shoulders. Even Marshal knew it meant that the man hadn't understood him.

"Okay," Marshal said slowly, "look at me." Marshal's eyes went back and forth between his hands and the man as he made fists and mimicked driving. "You got that, old man? I need a road outa here. To Marseilles." This he said as he both pointed away from the car, as well as made driving motions.

The man came closer to the car, but stood at the edge of the curb without stepping off. Mae, who had tried to remain disinterested in the conversation—knowing that whatever the man on the street told Marshal, he would ignore—looked past Marshal's shoulders to see the Italian. His long emotionless face fell into a white linen buttoned shirt, which hung off his shoulders. The sleeves landed in heaps at his wrists. His pants were some color of dark that caused Mae to think of grapes before they were turned to wine. She couldn't see his feet, but knew his shoes would make an impression as well. Mae found that she could not look away.

The Italian stretched out his left arm, with his index finger pointing seemingly toward the sky. He said a judicious "Autostrada," and did not speak again, just stood there pointing.

Marshal tried to follow the direction of the man's finger with his eyes, but could only see a hillside inlaid with terraced villas. And as if looking at the beautiful scene was more than his simple, agitated mind could take, Marshal's head began a small quake on top of his body. "Thanks a goddamn much!" he shouted to the man as he placed the car in gear and sped off, oblivious to the honking traffic around him. Mae's eyes never left the Italian. As she peered out the rear window of the car, she saw him mouth the word "Prego." Marshal had not thanked the man; she wanted to say something to the old man, to, once again, make excuses for Marshal.

"That wasn't very nice," she said as she turned to Marshal.

"What?"

"You know, the way you talked to that man. He looks like he could be somebody's ailing father, maybe your father, my father, anybody's father."

"Ha!" Marshal's laugh flew out the window. "That old mountain goat could never be my old man. And what the fuck, Mae? You don't even have a father."

"I mean..."

"Yeah, I know what you meant. You always got something to say don't you? No matter if it makes sense or not. I wish you'd help me get the fuck out this town! It was your idea to 'drive through Genoa,' Goddamit."

"I just meant, couldn't you be nicer to people, that's all." Mae wanted to remind him that she had been helping him all morning but he would not listen. And it was she who had warned him not to drive through the city in the first place. So much for the shortcut.

At the next corner, Marshal slid halfway into a parallel parking spot next to a corner market. There was a group of prostitutes and transvestites on the corner who took on the appearance of a litter of sex-starved alley cats. As Marshal got out of the car, they sidled up to him, purring their prices, stroking his ego up and down, and brushing their bodies as close to him as they could get. Marshal soaked up the attention, even bothered to pinch one of the females on her barely covered nipple.

Mae, at witnessing the scene, didn't become annoyed, just sat in the car staring ahead like she was in a trance.

After talking with the standing litter, Marshal bought a small bottle of water from the store—which he was already guzzling as he came out—and a magazine. As he climbed back into the car he threw the magazine at Mae and said, "I'm sure you can read that magazine a lot better than you can read a map."

Mae ducked her head just in time and the magazine landed in her lap, right side up, and ready to be read. "Well, at least you brought me something," she said. As they drove off, Marshal's new friends stood waving, with their fake hair falling down their backs. The kitteny professionals had given Marshal great directions. After a few right turns, Marshal found the main road out. "Give me a few hours and we'll be there," he said.

Mae didn't care. By now, she was so tired of being in the car with him. She turned her head towards the window, seeking solace from her surroundings, but every curve Marshal took as he raced down the carved mountainous road forced her back to him. An imploding rage was beginning to boil within her, even if there was no outlet for it. She tried to stare an angry hole into him. She looked at his chiseled unshaven face and he seemed outlandish to her in those moments. She saw his rigid eyes fighting with the roadway before him. She wondered how she could see beauty in those eyes, in him. She wondered if he would miss her if she threw herself out of the car. Would another car strike her into a simpler, gentler existence? Would he keep driving up and down those hills until he noticed she was no longer there? Would he drive on, after realizing that he had not missed her at all, that he did not need her in his life? Mae wanted to close her eyes on the possibility, but she was afraid that if she did, when she opened them again, her whole life would have to change; she would have to change.

She twisted back and forth—it felt as though the biggest of her life's decisions was sharing the seat with her. The wind burst through the open window and whipped her hair across her round face. The sun was so hot she felt the rays were literally baking her. The bottoms of her arms stuck to the magazine still lying in her lap—a layer of warm sweat crept between the seat and the underside of her thighs. She felt delirious, the breeziness enveloping and controlling her movements. To keep from falling asleep, she turned to the magazine.

Tina Turner was on the cover. Although Mae couldn't understand the language, from the pictures she guessed that the article focused on the house Tina had purchased in some town called Ville-France on the Cote d' Azur. She flipped through the pages of the magazine, trying to find the article on Tina. Maybe there was a picture of Tina's house, she thought. She had always thought of Tina as family—not real family, but she was sure they were related in spirit. In junior high, Mae had lip-synched to Tina's "Better Be Good to Me" for a talent show. She was a hit, especially with the boys. She smiled to herself as she remembered strutting across the stage of the school auditorium. She had been proud of her performance. She got backstage and found Jimmy Wills—with his arms stretched high, clapping over and over and over, and throwing his devious smile at her. The memory angered Mae. She was agitated at having thought of Jimmy—how could he have approached her at the talent show after what had happened? And why was she thinking of him now, on this trip, over twenty years later? Talking to Marshal didn't seem so bad all of a sudden.

"Marshal, Tina Turner bought a house in some town near Nice. Did you know that?"

"No, Mae. I didn't know." Sarcastically, and in no way interested.

"Yeah, she did. I was thinking… maybe we could go take a look at it. It's sorta on our way."

Shouting: "Have you lost your mind?"

"No."

"We're already late. I told Dizzy we'd be there by noon, and it's way after that now!"

"I know, but… we never do anything I want. I didn't even want to come on this asshole trip of yours."

"Well, you should have said something before I hauled your ass all the way up here, Mae."

"Screw you, Marshal."

"What did you say?"

Mae turned her head into the open window and said softly, "Screw you."

And as though he couldn't resist the small round head sticking out from the seat, Marshal whacked the back of Mae's head with his hand, sending her chin into the edge of the car door. Mae clutched at her face and turned further away from him. One tear fell. It landed on the top of her hand and disintegrated like a raindrop falling on a mushroom.

Trying not to cry, Mae found herself drifting in and out of a dreamy sleepiness mixed with indelible memories. Tina's house. Jimmy. That day in the woods …

Mae: So, Tina, tell us about this beautiful palace you live in.

Tina: Well, I could, but let me show you. I find it easier to talk as we walk around, okay?

Mae: Sure, I am in your hands now.

Tina: I did all the decorating myself. (Tina waves her slender fingers in the air, showing off a large living area with handpicked art, re-upholstered exotic print furniture, and a dark centerpiece coffee table that mirrors Tina's reflection as she passes by.)

Mae: How did you do it? I mean, you've just come off tour, right?

Tina: Yes, but a minor obstacle. I've always dreamed of this house, so when I found it, things seemed to fall into place. I shopped on my days off; I picked up little nuggets wherever I found them. My phone bill was enormous, as you can imagine. I saw to every detail even when I was thousands of miles away, darling.

Mae: Oh, Tina! (Breathlessly, stepping onto a spacious balcony. In the distance the city of Nice and the Mediterranean Sea are beyond). This is absolutely perfect. (Mae wonders what it would feel like to lie on one of the earth-colored chaises that lean against the stone pillars.) If only I could stay. Oh, Tina.

All those years before… although her mother told her never to walk home through the woods that surrounded the school, Mae had taken to doing just that. Secretly, she hoped she would meet someone there. But for weeks nothing happened, and on this particular day, as she etched her way through the forest, she felt calm and almost giddy. The sun sent the shadows of tall, leaning pines and strong, live oak trees stretching across her path as she walked along. This was perfection to her, pure and simple.

Mae prided herself in seeing beauty in everything. Therefore, when she saw an errant flower stuck in a bushel of weeds, she bent down to rescue it. But when she looked up, Jimmy Wills was standing before her with one hand in his pocket. She stared into a pair of young eyes that seemed very old just the same. His striped shirt had become untucked and hung down over his worn denim jeans. He looked down on her as though she was dead and he was there to give her new life.

"What are you doing here?" she asked.

"Looking for you, silly. I been lookin' for you all day. Where you been?"

She didn't understand him. It was incomprehensible that Jimmy would be looking for her. She stood up, and thought—briefly—about hurrying on home. Jimmy was smiling at her like she was his new treasure. Then he started pushing her toward an old tree that stood near. When her back touched the husky surface of the tree, his hands were already searching her chest, moving up and down and pinching her barely formed breasts. Mae wanted to tell him that he wouldn't find anything there; she was still waiting for the breasts that some of her female classmates already had in abundance. But Jimmy didn't seem to care.

"Kiss me," he told her.

Her eyes studied chapped lips that appeared to have small bite marks on them, and she recoiled. She thought of a snake ready to strike.

"Go ahead," he said, and nudged her arm.

So she let her lips pull the rest of her body over to Jimmy. Then his lips were smashing against hers. Only moments, but it seemed longer to Mae. She was about to tell Jimmy that she had to go; that her mother would be waiting for her to help cook. Jimmy lifted her dress and slid a hand down her underwear. "Oh," she whispered into the air.

"Lie down," he told her, reclaiming his hand from under her dress.

"I don't know, Jimmy."

"Just lie down like I told you."

Mae sat down by a patch of mushrooms. Jimmy kneeled down in front of her, and seeing that she wasn't going to go down on her own, he pushed her. When she fell back she felt the round heads give way beneath her.

Jimmy pushed his hands up until he found the band of her panties again. He pulled. Mae flinched, and drew her legs closer together. Jimmy pulled on the panties until he managed to get them down her legs, then left them in a heap at her ankles. He unleashed his belt and slid down the zipper of his pants. Mae turned her head away as Jimmy's body fell on her. The force made her cough, once. She searched the little bunches of weeds cropping up over the area. She wondered if there were other flowers caught like the one she had just freed. Jimmy was moving his bottom up and down, up and down. She wondered if she was supposed to feel anything. Her legs remained closed, and other than Jimmy's weight upon her, she didn't feel any different. She looked down to see the top of his head making jerking movements. His hair needed combing, she thought to herself. And he smelled like a chicken caught in the rain. Her mother always said boys smelled funny. "That's one reason you need to stay away from them," her mother would say.

"Mmn, I guess it's true," Mae said.

"What?" said Jimmy, as he stopped what he was doing. "What's true?"

"Oh, nothing. I was just thinking to myself."

"Well, you might wanta stop thinkin'; you're messin' up my concentration."

"Okay." And then, "Jimmy?"

"What now?

"I was thinking, maybe I oughta get home. My Mama's gonna be extra mad at me if I'm not there to help her cook."

"Dog blammit, Mae! Can't your mother cook by herself?"

"Yeah, she can."

"So, why you gotta be there?"

"I don't got to. I don't mind cooking. And Mama's got somebody stopping by. She probably need help."

Jimmy rolled off Mae onto his side, suddenly uninterested in his concentration. "How come y'all always got so many different cars parked in front of your house? What, are y'all feedin' everybody?"

"No, we ain't feedin' everybody, just one or two of Mama's friends sometimes."

"Oh, so that's it."

"Yeah."

Mae pulled up her underwear and got up to go, leaving Jimmy still lying on the ground.

"You wanta do this again?" he asked her.

"I don't know, Jimmy. I don't think I ought to." Then she turned and went home to her mother.

Mae didn't see Jimmy Wills at school the next day so that when she walked through the woods, she didn't have to wonder whether or not he would follow her. For some reason she didn't think he'd come the next day either. But just as she got halfway through the woods, she saw two figures approaching her—the smaller figure was Jimmy, the bigger one Jimmy's older brother, Big Wills. As they got closer, she could see that they weren't smiling. Her nervous smile left, too.

"Looky here, Mae," Jimmy was the first to speak. "I come to finish what I got started the other day, you know what I mean?"

Mae's eyes ran up and down Jimmy, then jumped over to Big Wills. "So, what's he doing here?"

"He my brother, girl." Jimmy tilted his head towards Big Wills.

"I was tellin' him how nice you was, and he wanted to come see for hisself. You ain't got no problem with that do you?"

"Jimmy, I ain't got time for… ," she started saying, but knew it was irrelevant because Jimmy and Big Wills stood there looking at her with an awful spirit in their eyes.

Big Wills stepped up, planting himself directly in front of her. "I'm afraid you're gonna have to make time for us 'cause we ain't leavin, and you ain't leavin' till we do."

Mae looked up, and up, till she found Big Will's face. He was so much taller than she. She noticed bits of hair starting to grow around the under edges of his puffy round chin.

She felt the hair on one of his arms barely touch the side of her face. She didn't think of running, of saving herself from what this half-grown man would do to her, but instinctively she knew she needed to go, and quickly. Her history and math books tumbled to the ground as she bolted. Then Mae was running, running faster and with more purpose than she had ever run. She could barely feel her feet as they touched the ground. She could hear Jimmy and Big Wills' breath sounds as they chased her. Jimmy's sounded like he was wheezing. Big Wills' like he was munching on something awful tasting.

When she saw the edge of the woods coming up, she knew she would be free of Jimmy and his man-like brother. The glare off some object served to both blind and propel her towards it. "Run!" the shiny object said, "Run!"

She felt the sting of Big Will's hand just before he actually clamped down on her shoulders. The force with which he tackled her made her fall so hard, so piercingly hard, that she felt it in all of her teeth. Her progress stopped, but she ran on, her legs rotating, fighting the air. Then Big Wills was on top of her, rolling her onto her back, hitting her across the face with his fists. His hands moved downwards intermittently to find her throat and choke her for a few moments before he began to strike her face again. Mae's head jounced back and forth against a shadowy patch of ground.

Jimmy, who had caught up to them by then, pulled on Big Will's arms until he stopped. "What are you doing, man? Come on, we gotta get outa here!"

Mae heard them move away and then disappear into the light of the fading afternoon. She wanted to move but couldn't. It was like a painful sleep from which she could not awaken…

"Wake up, Mae." Marshal was shaking her. "Come on, wake your ass up."

"Okay, okay!"

"Well, get your things together. We'll be there soon."

Mae struggled to sit up in the seat, and remembered they were going to Marseilles to meet up with Marshal's friend. "Tell me again why I have to meet this guy," she said.

"Come on, Mae. What's wrong with you? You still upset about before. Look, I'm sorry. But you know you had it coming."

"Yeah, Marshal, I had it coming." She waited. He said nothing. So she pushed. "I'm getting tired of this, Marshal."

"Oh, fuck. Here we go again."

"I'm serious, Marshal."

"Unh, huh."

"Did you know I was almost raped when I was just a girl? I was dreaming about it just now." She waited for any sign of sympathy.

"What?" Only incredulous stupor.

"Yeah, by this boy named Jimmy Wills and his brother."

"What do you mean 'almost'?"

"The brother beat me up, left me in bad shape. I eventually got another beating from my mother because I shouldn't 'a been putting myself out there like that."

"Like what, Mae? Nobody asks to be raped."

"It doesn't matter. It's just strange that I'd dream of that now, on this trip with you." She looked out the window and saw that the stacked cliffs of northwestern Italy had given way to open fields, tracts of lush green farms and wineries surrounded by rows of purplish grapes clinging to old tree-like vines. The scene made her think of the old Italian in Genoa, and this somehow gave her courage. "I can't go on like this anymore. Are you hearing me, Marshal?"

He ran the back of two fingers along the side of her moist face and flashed a surprisingly soft smile. The gesture felt tender to Mae. "Okay," he said, "I'm hearing you." She almost believed him.

When they reached the hotel, Marshal ran up to find his friend's room, leaving Mae waiting, leaning with her back against the parked, still-steaming car. Her eyes wandered about nervously. She felt as if everyone was watching her: the passing motorists, the tourists in the parking lot, the so-called rude French people in their beautiful, cozy houses, and now, even the man standing on the balcony with Marshal. When they saw her take notice of them, they waved her up. When she didn't come, they started down the stairs, one after the other, like lumberjacks going to cut down trees. They drew closer, and her mind began to jump. She stood erect, tensing, struggling to breathe naturally. With every step the two men made, her mind moved further and further back in time, until it was twenty years earlier and it wasn't Marshal and his friend that were walking towards her; it was Jimmy and Big Wills. She could still see their awkward yet determined movements as they closed in on her. Jimmy's eyes glistened with expectation. Big Will's looked settled—his mouth was closed, with one lip wrapped over the other, with anticipation. Big Wills reached out his right hand to her, almost as though he meant her no harm. It was his warped smile that told her to run, to run faster than she had ever run. In many ways, she now realized, she was still running. But why hadn't she found a better way of living her life? Her mind was beginning to question, to work things out. But then Marshal was standing beside her, with his arm closing around her waist. He squeezed ever so gently in the way that Mae had grown accustomed to, and he said, "This is my Mae." His friend was reaching his hand out to her. Looking around, everything seemed quiet, perfect even. But instinctively, something told her to run.

3. Bus People

Jillie stares at two of the bus people: a set of twin sisters. These two hold her attention because they are women, passing middle age, and appear to have been soldered by time. They also look mentally challenged in some way. It's something about their teeth, which protrude, and the calm smile coating their faces. They must be sweet people, but they are strange to Jillie. She begins to feel sad about all the things she cannot know about the women's lives. She wants to go back to her childhood and, while tugging on her mother's arm, ask her, "What's wrong with those women, Mommy? Why are they clinging to each other so closely?"

As Jillie is working out these things in her head, another woman boards the bus. She is abundantly large, and carries herself like she is a rack of lamb—carefully because she knows she is valuable and yet, she will throw herself onto the seat because she knows she is sturdy enough not to bruise. She sees the twin women, who are sitting up front in the elderly and handicapped section of the bus—where there is adequate room and where the passengers stare at each other. Usually the seats are taken up by youngsters who are too lazy to trek to the back of the bus, or by women holding or escorting her babies or small children. So the large, extensive woman decides, as if by premonition, that she will sit with the twins. Her girth plops down in between them, squeezing them apart and causing them to shudder slightly. Jillie sees it, if no one else does. The twins scoot over, uncomfortably, as if they are now sitting on a warming pan. The woman turns and looks at each, first right then left, and nods her head as if to say, "Now we're in business." Jillie thinks everything should be okay, or at least bearable, meaning that the universe should move along peaceably. She even begins to turn her attention to other passengers on the bus. Although there are always odds and ends types of people, ones Jillie can take up in her imagination when she is bored, today there seems to be none. Everyone is either dressed nicely, obviously on their way to work, like Jillie, or are school teenagers and other locals who must get somewhere on this warm spring morning.

"Ow!" someone says suddenly. Jillie looks in the twin women's direction. The twin on the opposite side of the large woman appears on the verge of crying. Her face is puffy with hidden rage, which offers its own version of redness. The other twin is peering around the large woman's body trying to ascertain what has happened to her sister. Both twins are wearing different colors of one of those sports hats—you know, the round floppy kind that doddering old fishermen wear. The hats look good on the sisters, but Jillie is finding it hard to truly see their faces. The concerned twin is almost up on her feet; clearly, she wants to go to her sister and comfort her, or at least ask her what is wrong. Jillie realizes that there is something tender and natural about the way such people are: their innocence is palpable. There is nothing abstract about it. You can see it in everything that they do. This makes other people either love them unconditionally or hate them, who knows, based on these other people's inadequacies. Jillie cannot fathom what the large woman could have done, but she knows she has done something. This is why Jillie places her attention on the woman and leaves it there.

The buffalo-sized woman probably senses Jillie's eyes on her, and she turns and stares back, as if to say, I will not back down. Jillie sees for the first time that the woman has about three chins hanging down her face. That must be difficult, Jillie thinks. The woman also has small lips, or perhaps they just seem small because her cheeks are so wide. Jillie thinks the woman's face could be that of a flounder, especially with that teeny nose poking out. The woman's hair lands in light brown strings upon her shoulders. Even the woman's dress is unappealing: it appears to once have been one color but has been washed by the sun into a duller version, say from pumpkin orange to graying yellow. Jillie notices something else, something that may define the woman most: she has sad, sad eyes. Jillie can almost see the pain that is locked inside them. Jillie imagines the life this woman has led—one where she has had little, if any, control. Jillie looks into the woman's past and sees long days of abuse—abuse that starts at a young age, perhaps when the woman is only six or seven. The men who come to the widowed mother's home, the boys who sit next to her on darkened buses or even in classrooms near the back and who place their hands inside her panties and fondle what is young and unprotected. Jillie sees the young girl begin to lose herself, because who is there after all to help her or to tell her that she has the power to say no. So the years pass and she becomes someone not resembling the self she was supposed to be, taking on instead the unhappy role of harming others who she thinks are weak, like her. Jillie sees all this as she stares at the oversized woman sitting at the front of the bus, separating innocent twin sisters who only seem to have each other in the world. At some point, staring seems pointless, so Jillie backs off.

The twins have settled down. At the very least, Jillie has managed to give the one some moments of peace. Then Jillie sees the larger woman pushing herself into the twin—in miniscule, barely noticeable drops of abuse, the woman is sliding her enormous body into the twin who is nearly hidden from Jillie's view. Soon, another "Ow!" The twin is beginning to moan as well. It is as though her speech is gone. The other twin is up from her seat now. She stands in front of her sister and they communicate in their way. One hand finds another. Their eyes connect and they speak; it has become the language of the abused. When the twin, the one who has been pinched into the seat, stands up, Jillie is not surprised. Together, the sisters have chosen to remain standing rather than accept the torturous ride. They move away from the row of seats and stand holding on to each other in the aisle—one of them is now next to Jillie. She looks over at the large woman, now sitting alone, and sees how satisfied she looks. A smile actually escapes, or has she thrown it out there on purpose? Jillie becomes angry then. From her gut, she feels disgusted with the woman. If she could walk over and slap her, she would do so. Jillie thinks of what Toni Morrison says about women using the "weapons of the weak" to hurt and destroy other women. Why, she wonders, must women do that.

The twins are holding hands fully. They, too, look happier. Soon, they signal that they want to get off at the next stop. When the bus comes to a stop, the twins depart from the back. Jillie thinks they do so instead of passing the mean woman again. They are done with her and need never see her again. The woman is still interested in them, though. Her eyes follow them after they are off the bus. She and Jillie both see that the twins are walking toward the gates of a retirement home. Satisfied, the woman straightens herself in her seat. She plops her plump arms, crossed, upon her belly. She thinks she is fine with herself, no questions about that.

But Jillie cannot get the twin sisters out of her mind. For the rest of her bus ride, she wonders who the women are going to see in the retirement home. Their mother or father? A sister or brother? No, Jillie decides they are visiting a friend, someone who loves them because she wants to. She is like an older sister to them; she has helped them throughout their lives and now, when she is no longer able to consistently care for herself, the twins come and visit every day. They bring joy to this woman's life. Yes, Jillie thinks, this is who the twins are and why they would punish themselves with such a bus ride.

When Jillie's stop comes around, she purposefully departs from the front of the bus. As she passes the large woman who has caused certain pain and disruption in the twin sisters' lives, Jillie stops briefly and shakes her finger, as if to say, there is no justification for her behavior.

The woman is not changed by this. Jillie's actions don't appear to even register with her. And yet, Jillie leaves the bus feeling stronger. She decides that from now on she will get off the sidelines of life, that she will stop being just the observer; she will speak up. The next time she will get outside of her head; she will act. Her feet touch the pavement, and briskly, she moves toward the building where she works.

Girl Watcher

Jerry followed the young woman into Popeye's. He had not been inside the popular food chain in many months, and the overbearing smell that greeted him as he walked through the door reminded him of why he didn't like fast food. He could afford to eat at the finer restaurants New Orleans had to offer. And yet, here he was standing in line at Popeye's, only a few steps behind the young woman he had followed in. A young Vietnamese family stood between Jerry and the young woman. Two little girls with thick dark hair hung off either side of their mother, or her handbag, or they twirled around, each trying to outperform the other as a ballerina. Jerry would have suffered these antics any other day; the little girls were, after all, what he considered pretty: their small, slightly puffy faces showing no signs of losing baby fat or growing tougher jaws. Every time they looked up at Jerry, their eyes sparkled for him. Today, though, the little cuties annoyed the hell out of him, mostly because he was intent on observing the young woman he was following, without being detected by her. The children were getting dangerously close to bumping into the girl. As it was, Jerry feared the young woman would see him—through the wall of twirling action—recognize him, and then this little game he was playing would be over.

After several close calls—when the girls actually fell against the back of the young woman's legs; thank God, not on purpose—Jerry realized that he should not have worried. The young woman would not turn around no matter what the children did. The several apologies that the mother sent up to her may as well have been tossed in with the chicken being thrown into the vat of oil. The young woman neither turned to acknowledge the mother's pitifully spoken words, nor did she throw a paltry "That's okay" over her shoulders. She stood with her hands at her sides, all zombie-like, or like she'd been drugged, forced to stand in line and wait to order chicken. Thanksgiving was weeks away, and Jerry imagined the young woman alone on such a holiday; she gave off that kind of scent: lonely and easily taken advantage of. The sweater she wore was tattered at one of the elbows—clearly overused; Jerry pictured her wearing it everywhere she went. Jerry had begun to feel sorry for her, envisioning her as someone who was poor and in need of him (or someone else) to take care of her. Even though he was clearly twenty years older than she, he knew he could be that person.

When her turn in line came, the young woman edged up to the counter, slower than any of the other people waiting in line thought possible. Jerry could not see her face, so he only imagined what was going on. The thirty-ish woman who stood behind the counter asked the young woman a second time, "May I take your order?" Jerry could see that if the young woman did not order something soon, the woman behind the counter would get upset. He did not want this to happen; what would happen to his plan of saving the girl if there was a scene in this place? Actually, such an affront to the young woman would be seen by him as improper and rude. Under normal circumstances, when he wasn't trying to go unnoticed by a young woman he was following around town, he would have yelled, "What's the rush? Give her a chance to order." He often thought of himself as being a keeper of civility, but on a day like this, he knew it went deeper. Jerry began to get anxious, understanding that he had few options. If the young woman didn't speak soon, the whole atmosphere of this chicken-and-biscuit-eating haven might burst into chaos. The young woman's head tilted up as though she were calling on a higher power. Jerry knew she was still perusing the menu, deciding what to order.

After what Jerry deemed an interminably long time, the young woman stepped closer to the counter. "I would like the four piece," she said, "with red beans and rice as a side."

"Would you like a drink with that?"

"Do you have root beer?"

"It's New Orleans, baby; we got Barq's."

This seemed a little rude to Jerry; he thought a simple "Yes, we do" would have sufficed.

"How about strawberry?" the young woman asked.

"Will that be regular, medium, or large?"

"Well..." she stuttered. "Maybe I'll take a root beer." Had the girl really changed her mind or was she fooling with the woman behind the counter? Jerry wondered. A smile grew on his face.

"That will be $8.69," the woman behind the counter said, without a moment's hesitation. She had obviously gotten used to all kinds of customers and their fickle habits.The young woman took a ten dollar bill from her wallet and pushed it close to the woman's face. The woman took the money and lowered it, decisively, as if she were showing the young woman where and how to move money from one person's hands to another's. Although he didn't know why, Jerry wondered if the Popeye's worker was having a good day. Briefly, he thought of different scenarios that would have planted the woman in such a job; surely, it hadn't been her life's goal to work at a fried chicken chain. Probably some stroke of bad luck, Jerry thought. He wanted to chide himself for thinking so, but he assumed there was a pretty good chance she had dropped out of school as a teenager, probably not much younger than this girl who Jerry was following. The sensible part of him said there were a myriad of reasons anyone ended up working at Popeye's or any other food chain: illness, teenage pregnancy, improper role models, but certainly it couldn't be by choice. As he stood there, he told himself not to judge the woman at the counter—to keep track of his real objective, this stunning young woman who had captured his imagination since he first saw her a couple of hours before. The young woman took the receipt and the change and pushed her tray down the counter. Luckily, the Vietnamese woman and her children took forever to order their meal: each child changed her mind several times before the mother settled the matter by ordering for them. "They'll both have the chicken strips," she said, to which the girls smiled and twirled their last dance for Jerry. By then, the young woman had received her order and had gone to the seating area.

Jerry dared not look in the young woman's direction. He contentedly kept his eyes forward until he had ordered and picked up his two piece dark from the counter. As he moved further down, to the soft drink dispenser, he pushed himself sideways, shuffling as though he were doing a two-step. After he had filled his cup with Coke, he turned, allowing only his eyes to move around the room, scanning for the young woman's location. At first he didn't see her, but as he moved further into the seating area, he saw that she had taken a seat on the opposite side of the room, close to the restroom. He needn't have worried about being spotted; she was busy pushing pieces of the fried chicken into her mouth—ripping it off the bones and packing her mouth as though she had not eaten in days.

The sight of the young woman devouring the food both endeared the girl to Jerry and sickened him at the same time. His mind went back to when he first saw her that morning at the breakfast restaurant. He would have easily noticed her even if she hadn't made several trips to the breakfast bar. She was one of those pretty bright-skinned black girls, passé blanche, with silky hair half down her back. She moved, supplanting each foot with the other. She seemed to Jerry a timid little flower taking too much time to bloom. After the third trip to the food bar—each time filling up her plate with bacon, sausages, biscuits and gravy, grits, dollar pancakes—Jerry began to notice more than the young woman's appearance. "What the hell is she doing with all that food?" Jerry had said to his friend, Allan.

Both he and Allan had been commenting on the girl's looks, trying to figure out how old she was. Jerry said she couldn't be more than sixteen, but Allan said he thought she was at least twenty. Either way, the men agreed that she was jail-bait for them. But what could it hurt to take a gander and imagine they were young again? All of the talk had gotten Jerry interested in a way he hadn't been for some time. This bi-weekly breakfast with his best friend was one of the few pleasures of his life. Even though his wife had died four years before, he couldn't imagine giving up his freedom, at least not for a while. He would wait and let the next woman come to him.

"I'm going to see who she's with," Jerry said to his friend. "The suspense is killing me."

Before his buddy could convince him to sit down, Jerry had gone to pick up a new plate and was headed to the far end of the food bar, where the fruit and an assortment of muffins were waiting. As he walked, he looked around the restaurant. Three booths down, he saw her. She set her napkin on the table then rose up, dusting crumbs from her lap. Jerry's mouth watered and he swallowed hard. He watched as the young woman moved away from the table and toward the restroom. He wondered for a moment if he could get away with following her there, if she'd notice him standing outside waiting when she exited. He placed his plate back on the stack of empties and walked toward the bathroom. There was a partition covering the entranceway to the two bathrooms. After Jerry was behind the make-shift wall, he knew he should continue and go into the men's room, but he found himself, instead, lingering in front of the ladies' restroom. He pressed his ear against the door.

He was completely surprised to hear the vomiting sounds ring out. There was no mistake; the girl was doing some serious puking inside. He jerked his head back, thinking that he had heard someone approaching. He waited a minute more, wishing for more acceptable sounds coming from the bathroom. He wanted to be sure of what he had heard. The girl's coughs ran over him in streams of revulsion. There was no mistake; she was in there regurgitating her food. There was nothing left to do but to return to his seat; he felt that he, too, might begin to throw up.

Back at his table, Jerry met Allan's stare and realized that he must look ridiculous to his friend. He could feel his face flush. He wanted to smile, but he felt sadder than he had in a long time. "I thought you were going to get some more food," Allan said.

Jerry returned the look in his friend's eyes with a sympathetic smile. He knew he wouldn't tell Allan what he had come to know about the girl. It would be his own secret, or his and the young woman's. Telling Allan would cheapen the whole idea of what she had begun to mean to him. The truth was that he knew Allan would make fun of her. He was sure of it.

When the young woman came to the food bar once again, Jerry found himself looking away. He didn't want to give the secret away, but he also wasn't sure of how he would react if she saw him looking at her. Allan kicked him under the table. Allan had a school boy's ignoble grin on his face. Jerry sent back a deceitful smile that he had dug up from his insides and that he found hard to project. He felt like a broken machine that no longer could do its job. He suddenly wanted this time-honored date with his friend to be over. "Hey, shouldn't we be getting out of here," he said.

"Sure, sure. I've got to pick up my kids in about half an hour."

"Okay."

"Just let me get a little fruit, and I'll be ready."

Jerry contemplated leaving his friend to eat alone. Allan was a notoriously slow eater. He never would have made it in the military, Jerry often told him. But Allan always threw it back in Jerry's face with, "Well neither would you." It was true. Jerry didn't want to follow in his dad's footsteps. And the truth is that he felt a little too privileged. His middle-class parents believed in a family's sitting down to dinner every day. No matter what he and his siblings were doing, they knew to be home at 7:00 p.m. The family would then take their time going through all the courses of food their mother (or their maid) had prepared. While they ate, they talked about politics and education and all those important things Jerry's father thought they should know. "No child of mine will be stupid," his father often said. His mother took pride in rebuffing Jerry's father with, "Well, I hope every child of mine is compassionate." Jerry's father, who had spent ten years in the navy before he went on to start his own business as a consultant, would stare Jerry's mother down, as though he were still in the military and he were dressing down one of his seamen.

So, proper etiquette, as well as upbringing, demanded that Jerry sit there and wait until his friend finished eating. Every so often, Jerry would glance over his shoulders to see if the young woman was still there, or whether or not she had made another run to the bathroom. The thought of it began to eat away at Jerry. He began to wonder what the young woman could be thinking. Why come to an all-you-can-eat breakfast bar if all she planned to do was throw it up? Jerry didn't completely understand the word Bulimia. He had heard the term before but couldn't imagine what would make a young woman behave in this way. All the girls he had known were strong eaters. You didn't have to ask them to eat.

As soon as Allan had stuffed down a couple of plates of strawberries, cantaloupe, and vanilla pudding, he sat back in his chair and, rubbing his stomach, said to Jerry, "Okay, let's get going."

Jerry had already placed his napkin over his plate and drained what was left of his coffee. He and Allan headed for the front of the restaurant to pay their bills. Jerry peered over to the young woman's booth as he walked. She wasn't there and the placemat and food were gone. Jerry assumed that she had left. He felt relieved; the thought of the girl eating more food was beginning to affect his equilibrium. Jesus, she's making me dizzy with all this, Jerry thought.

In the parking lot, Allan and Jerry parted, promising to call each other next week. Allan pulled away first, while Jerry fumbled with the glove compartment. When he finally got it open, he placed his receipt in a stack with the others, rewrapped everything with a large rubber band, and then tucked it back before locking the latch again.

When Jerry sat up in his seat, his eyes landed on the young woman coming out of the restaurant. She was pulling at her sweater. The day wasn't cold, but there was a small chill still. The sweater didn't have a zipper or a tie to keep it closed, so she folded her arms tightly across her chest and began to walk out of the parking lot. Jerry was surprised when she suddenly turned back and went directly to a bike that lay on the ground between two large hedges in front of the restaurant. She lifted the bike from the bushes and got on easily, using one leg to push off. Jerry watched as she gently pedaled away, down the street. He imagined himself moving on, driving off in the opposite direction as soon as she was out of sight. But, half a block down, he saw her turn into Popeye's, and without thinking about it, he found himself cranking up the Firebird and driving the short distance there. By the time he pulled into the lot, the young woman had already discarded her bike. There was no thought to tether the bike, or to lean it tenderly against a tree or some other firm surface. Jerry thought the bike was a nuisance to her, and she was gladly rid of it. He sat in the car, waiting for someone else to go into the restaurant. He couldn't be sure she hadn't seen him at the breakfast bar, and he wanted a buffer between them. He waited. In a few minutes, a Vietnamese woman and two young girls parked next to him then juggled themselves into Popeye's. Jerry could barely wait to follow.

He knew she couldn't see him when he sat down with his tray of food. He positioned himself against the back wall, facing her backside. Jerry had barely sat down when the young woman got up and walked calmly to the bathroom. Jerry wondered how someone could hold their composure so resolutely when, in moments, she was going to be in the bathroom, forcing all that food to come heaving up. How could she do it? Jerry looked down at his own food—the fried chicken, covered in grease, the dirty rice, sitting in its own film of oil. The only thing that now looked edible was the biscuit, and it, too, would probably upset his stomach later. For a moment, he considered opening up the soft buttered biscuit and spreading honey on it, but he thought of the young woman and what she was doing—he told himself that if he listened hard enough, he could hear her from where he sat—and all of it made him lose his appetite. He imagined not wanting to eat, ever again.

When she came out of the bathroom, Jerry waited to see if she would order more food. She didn't. She slipped out the door quickly, as if she were suddenly trying to escape her predicament. Jerry picked up the tray and tossed the food into the trash, then rushed outside. He caught sight of the girl riding down the street in the same direction she had been going before she decided to stop at Popeye's. He was able to follow her easily enough. The only other restaurants nearby were obviously out of the girl's price range, except for a McDonald's a few blocks down. He found himself hoping that she was going home or off to a friend's house to listen to music, or whatever young women did on Saturday mornings. From the distance, he could see the McDonald's arches glaring in the sky. "Please, please don't stop," he found himself saying. He had seen her at the Shoney's for most of the morning, and then at Popeye's as lunch was kicking off, but he had no way of knowing how long she had been making this tour of restaurants. There was a Burger King in the opposite direction and other restaurants blocks beyond that. The thought of all the possibilities worried Jerry. She could eat until she either passed out from exhaustion, or she ran out of money. And where would she get that kind of money, Jerry wondered. She's in tattered clothes; she can't have the money to do this. Jerry wanted to hang his head because he didn't know how much longer he could follow her along her disgusting journey.

To Jerry's despair, he watched as she rode her bike into the McDonald's parking lot. Again, she threw the bicycle aside and went rushing into the restaurant. Jerry parked his car but couldn't go in. He wouldn't go traipsing after her and play this game of hide and not seek, and then watch her gorge herself with, what, burgers and fries, and a strawberry milkshake? He sat in his car and waited. Even from the car, he could see her moving through the motions of her disorder—ordering food, the table near the bathroom, the food being pushed down her throat and then encouraged to come up again. Jerry thought of how ironic the whole exercise was, how difficult it was to get so much food down, and how easy it must seem to the young woman to stick her finger down her throat and have the food come rushing back up. He tried to remember the last time he had thrown up any of his food. He couldn't. He finally decided that he had never done such a thing, even as a child. No more than fifteen minutes passed and she was out of McDonald's, just as she had gone rushing from Popeye's. Jerry cranked his car, ready for whatever would come. He didn't realize it, but he had begun to pray. His mind kept it a tidy secret from him, but in his heart he was praying for the girl. As he followed her this time, he told himself that he would rush to the door of the next restaurant she stopped at, and he would demand that she stop, that she get some help. He knew he had no right to do this, but he felt it was his duty. A large part of him now felt as if he knew this young woman. It had gone so much further than he and Allan staring at her across the breakfast bar and making snide remarks about her being a "pretty little thing." He felt ashamed of being that person; he wanted to imagine that he could or had somehow changed since he'd first seen her. It wasn't very likely. After all, why would a thirty-eight year-old man suddenly feel responsible for a young woman he didn't know? Why should he feel responsible for changing this girl's life?

When she pedaled up to a corner grocery store, the girl brought her bike to a stop but didn't turn in. She placed her hands in her pockets and began counting her money. The grocery store probably served po-boys and hot sausages. The thought of hot sausages made Jerry want to throw up. Years before, he had been in homeroom hour just after lunch and one of his classmates had thrown up the hot sausage he had brought for lunch. Jerry remembered the awful pink, globby mess that had gone flying all over the table where he was sitting. For the longest time, he hadn't been able to eat hot sausages or hot dogs or anything that was wrapped in French bread and dressed.

To Jerry's relief, the young woman put the money back in her pocket, kicked off, and rode down the street. He followed her for several blocks until she turned onto a side street. These were some of the houses of old New Orleans, many of them having accommodated the best middle-class families for generations—all the yards were landscaped and shrouded by shady oaks. It had been a while, but Jerry thought the street could be the one that one of his classmates had lived on. He wondered briefly if the family still lived there.

The girl pedaled faster now, as though she were late for an appointment. Jerry kept his distance, not wanting to be found out at this stage. There were few other vehicles on the street. She eventually turned into a beautiful old double shotgun painted in bright colors and sitting high off the street. The street-level apartment beneath the house gave it an almost regal look. As Jerry parked a few houses down, he noticed the girl toss her bike aside and go past a wide set of steps. Large banana leaves swayed and courted her as she pushed past and went up the side stairs and into the door. Jerry was beginning to recognize the sheer coincidence of the situation he now found himself in. This was definitely his classmate's house, which meant this young lady was someone he could have met in his life. Looking up at the large picture window in the kitchen, Jerry hoped he could continue his surveillance of the girl. It wasn't long before he saw her placing plates and glasses and silverware on the table. You've got to be kidding me, Jerry thought. She was rushing to get home for lunch? Jerry felt like banging his head on the steering wheel just to make certain he was still sane. The girl looked happy enough. She went about her duties as though she had been called by a higher power. He could see her speaking to someone in the background, probably her mother finishing up the meal. The girl even laughed once, doubling over as though the joke was so funny she couldn't stand up straight. Jerry concluded that all of this had to be an act. He couldn't reconcile how the young woman he had been following that morning had suddenly turned into a joyous, doting daughter.

As Jerry watched and pondered the significance of the girl's behavior, a car drove up. A tall mulatto man almost crawled out of the Volvo he was driving. Even from the distance of the years since Jerry had seen him, and two yards that separated them now, Jerry recognized the man as his old classmate, Eddie Batiste. Jerry leaned over, reaching for his glove compartment, as though he were looking for something—hoping that Eddie would not see him. Moments passed and Jerry began to feel safe. He kept his eyes buried in the car, even when he had opened the compartment. He found that none of this helped when Eddie came knocking at his door.

"Is that you, old buddy," Eddie said. He bent down and cupped his hands against the window, trying to get the best view of Jerry inside.

Jerry realized that he couldn't hide. He prepared himself for the customary greeting he would give his old friend.

"I can't believe my eyes. Is that you, Eddie?" Jerry kept his hands in the glove compartment, hoping to convince Eddie of what he had been doing.

"It's me. Is that you, Jerry?"

"It's me," Jerry returned, completing the old way they had of kidding around. Both men broke into semi-laughs, their smiles like giant welcome mats to the other.

"Well, get out, man. What you doing?"

"I was just looking for a receipt. I got something I need to return to Schwegmanns. I pulled off on this street, not thinking you used to live over here." By this time, Jerry had closed and locked the latch of the glove compartment and was getting out of the car. He didn't want Eddie looking too closely.

"Yeah, still here. My folks died some years back and me and my wife and our daughter moved here. My brother's in Texas and sister's got her own place. Someone had to move in here, know what I mean?" Eddie nudged Jerry in the side then.

"Yeah, sure do. I'm still trying to pay a mortgage, myself."

"Where you at, now, man?"

"Still over in Gentilly."

"Yeah?"

"Yeah."

"Wow, man, you got kids?"

"No. . . that your daughter?" Jerry pointed at the window, where the young woman now sat looking out the window, at Jerry and her father talking.

"Yep, that's my Hillary. You wouldn't believe she's almost seventeen, next month."

"No?" Jerry said, now sure he was a pervert. He recovered: "It don't seem like we been out of school that long. When'd you get married?"

"Right after we graduated."

"To who? I know her?"

"Nah, I doubt it. Met her the first day at LSU. She kept, but college didn't. Dropped out after I hurt my knee and the scholarship money stopped. How 'bout you?"

"Yeah, I finished. My old man made sure."

"Rode your ass, huh?"

"Yeah, but it wasn't so bad, you know?"

"Yeah, I wish my old man had been tougher on me. Nah, let me stop lying. I wasn't gonna finish college anyhow. After me and Adrienne got married, we worked for a few years trying to save up money for a house, then the girl came, and we kinda let things slide."

"Having kids makes it hard, eh?"

"You never married?"

"Yeah, to Lisa. Remember she was all impressed and shit 'cause I was a Saint Aug. man?"

"Fuck me! You married her, man?"

"Yeah."

"Don't downplay it, man. That girl was hot back then; she's probably triple hot now, right?"

"Yeah, she was. She died about four years back."

"Fuck, man. Sorry to hear it. What happened?"

"Cancer."

"Man, that sucks, yeah."

"Yeah."

"Listen, why don't you come in? Adrienne got me coming home for lunch instead of spending money at all them fast food restaurants. It's better for me. Gotta keep this figure." Eddie ran his hand down the front of his body, over a round belly.

Jerry laughed. He found himself happy to be in his old classmate's presence. He briefly thought back to the days when he was seventeen, eighteen, just getting out of school, his whole life before him. God were things so fucking simple, and yet, he always thought his whole world was about to fall apart.

Jerry looked up at the window and remembered why he had come here in the first place. Could he go into Eddie's house and watch the man's daughter scarf down more food and then disappear from the table to complete the morning's ritual? Could he sit there and eat and say nothing? Or would he become so outraged that he'd have to explain what the girl had been doing all morning?

The questions moved through Jerry's mind. What about the girl? Was he certain he had a duty to try and set her life right? To find out what was making her want to destroy herself? And what if he did say something to Eddie and he didn't believe him? What if he did? What would Eddie say about Jerry following his teenaged daughter from restaurant to restaurant? Jerry didn't know what he would do until Eddie patted him on the back and said, "Come on, man. We could use the company."

That's when Jerry imagined that what was ailing this young woman might be what was ailing this entire little family. There had to be something eating away at them—perhaps from the inside, perhaps something so big and shameful that the only way for Jerry to find out was to investigate it for himself. He told himself all these things, even though he wasn't sure of what he believed. He only knew that he had always wanted to know things, to get to the bottom of a mystery. He didn't know how he would figure it all out, but he thought he would go on faith.

Without thinking about it any further, Jerry turned to his old classmate and said, "Sure thing, Eddie. I could use a home-cooked meal."

The Strength of a Woman

It is only by summoning up all their strength and helping one another with loving care that human beings are able to maintain themselves at a tolerable height above the infernal abyss toward which they gravitate. They are joined together by ropes, and it is a bitter thing when the ropes around one of them slacken and he sinks a little lower than the others into the void, and it is quite horrible when the ropes around one of them break, and he then falls. That is why we should always hold on to other people. I incline to the belief that the girls sustain us because they are so light; that is why we have to love the girls and why they should love us.

—*Franz Kafka, 1903*

Rachel– 1984

She is thinking of Donnie and the way his life just quit hers. He had been a good friend of her brother—that's actually how they met.

It is a day when she comes to a fork in her life's road—how a woman must move on if a man is to be taken from her, by her own neglect.

A lover's response: an intimate scene with a woman lying on her side, not-so-peacefully naked and looking away, with her lover looking on. Will he come to her this time, even knowing that she could send him away with just her eyes?

Which beginning shall we use? They are each succinctly qualified.

Begin with the kiss.

She remembers it, the way he kissed her—like a full-grown man, or what she then suspected a man's kiss should be like. His lips, moist and barely toughened by the years, almost enveloped hers. She remembers her teeth, firmly confined as the suction of his breath pulled at the insides of her mouth. Strangely enough, she felt then, really felt it, that he was taking some of her with him—some of her youth, as though he was hungry in that way and needed her nourishment.

He was so much older at twenty-eight. He stood over her, a big man, tall and built as if from human sticks and stones. His skin was a brown to envy but rough and prickly against her face. She remembers her hands grabbing at his arms, trying to hold on; they felt like steel must feel before it bends, like something hot when it touches something cold.

He almost lifted her off the carpeted surface. As it was, her feet were arched like a ballet dancer's, her toes pointing into the living room floor. She submitted to the kiss willingly, allowing her own soft breath to mingle with his.

She thought of the kiss so often thereafter. And when, not a month later, even less, she learned of his death, she felt that she had been betrayed by the kiss, by his hazy and distant interest in her. Why, she should have asked, but instead decided that it had not mattered. He had not come again, to kiss her, or whatever it is that a man might have wanted to do to a teenaged girl who could not resist him.

He had said, "You're a tease, with your light-colored skin and your long, girl's hair. You'd want a man to get used to you, wouldn't you? And you know I could." Yet he had not come again. Not even with her brother to sit outside just after early dark and smoke Kool cigarettes and swat the mosquitoes away until it became so dark and so late that neither could see each other's smoky brown face, only their white teeth and the sound of their voices, which rarely died down.

He had also said that she had eyes that were special gifts from God, and that he didn't want her to look at him with them.

That's what she remembered when he was dead. She didn't cry at first, not upon hearing about the horrible accident. The tears came late one night, after the boys' team had lost its first basketball game of the season, and all the cheerleaders had cried then. She wet her pillow with tears that seemed too hot to be flowing from her cold body.

She cried then because she was relieved. That's what her best friend had said the next day, when she too had learned of his death. Her friend had remembered the day of the kiss differently.

"When he kissed you, Rachel," she said, "I thought you had become someone else. You called on the phone, and I could feel your excitement brush up against me as though we were standing right next to each other. I knew you liked him, mostly 'cause you were so afraid—afraid to be evil and afraid not to be."

She had stopped her friend then because she knew she was telling the true side of it all—the story, her existence in it. She knew she should be telling it herself. The beginning of her story would have to be told.

She said to her friend, "I thought he would ruin me, with that one kiss." She hadn't learned then, nor since, that she didn't need the safety net she had instinctively thrown around herself, below her, always, in those days, and in her adult years, so aware of any possible danger lurking, even in a kiss.

And now, as she sits in her favorite chair, still in her night clothes, her fine skin still smooth though it is twenty-five years older and beginning to grow wrinkles. She says, to herself, "My husband won't come near me." She is like some delicately crafted object just waiting to be taken up and admired by him. She is open, waiting to meet his embrace. Most days she can't bear to see him, for her eyes to meet his and for them to share their first kiss in many weeks.

This time he comes though, with a dream as an offering to her. With his hand on her arm, he begins. But he must talk to her back, for she does not turn from the open window.

"Just now," he says, "I was dreaming of you. You walked up a hill to where I stood, waiting. All the trees were green and the leaves hung lower than I've ever seen. I think the wind was blowing as well. Your hair was darker and longer, and it gently brushed your shoulders as you walked. When you reached me, we looked at each other as though there was no one else, and would be no one else, ever. I don't think I'd seen you the way I saw you then. Your face was so honest and pure; I guess I mean that it was your smile that was so pure, so innocent.

"And then we talked, as usual, but you tried to tempt me with a question that was long and tedious but would require that I think only of you. As you spoke, I could feel myself being seduced by you—but I knew I wouldn't let it be so. Instead of telling you what you wanted to hear—that I would walk past all the restrictions barring us from a total love, even this thing in the past, this man that you have tried to forget but cannot—instead of simply choosing to grab you up tightly in my arms, instead of doing these things, I simply allowed my head to touch yours, our foreheads, I mean. We stood there connected, just for a moment. I could feel you breathing softly; I thought at first that you would be out of breath. I knew this was our time, that life was being sucked back into us. And I knew this was a chance that wouldn't come again. When I woke up, it didn't feel like a dream at all. You had gotten up during the night. And here you sit."

The telling of the dream was over. He had said it; she had heard it. And that would have to be enough.

Mother Nature– 1959

The words, indeed, cut through his throat like the roar of a furnace on a cool, hushed winter evening. "Caught up in my bones, like FIRE! Like FIRE!"

And the whittled splinters of screams that come from him do not stop: "FIRE! I SAID FIRE!" With each word, his right foot comes down hard against the boarded floor beneath him, and his congregation—his attentive members—can hear the faint rippling of the water below. The more his foot comes down, the more the water shakes and turns into a shuddering force beneath him. One could almost imagine small waves splashing, in small tumults, against the sides of the pool.

The church is old, built a hundred and eighty years before. A pool had been built beneath the pulpit, a measure thought necessary to baptize the church's new members—a large sum then, often totaling ten or more each month—without having to trek the entire congregation to the local river for the baptizing service. The pool was built, and a platform was built around it—with wide, long and strong floorboards placed over the pool, boards which could be removed much like the floor of a modern day gymnasium and elevated to a height just below the congregation's line of vision.

"And then I can't move my feet," the preacher continues. "I'm standing like a fool that has no direction." And yet, his body moves, swaying back and forth. His is a very large frame, and it towers above the altar. Sweat settles at the sides of his temples rather than sliding down his face and onto his silk robe. He occasionally takes a well-folded handkerchief and swats at his swollen face. His dark head isn't completely fat but rather cheeky and sits obstinately on his shoulders instead of on a visible neck. One does not readily notice this because his deeply rolling, cadencing voice is carried unfettered out over the church pews, touching everything living and breathing there, and keeping it captive. It is his voice that can't be shaken.

"I done forgot the Lord," he says. "Some of you, too. For way too long. But you see, he KNOWS me." And the silk-robed man in the pulpit leans forward; his head seems to kiss the Bible, which lays open on the podium.

"Ha! Ha! He KNOWS me!" And his figure straightens. His arms are at his side, but then he spreads them up like wings as if he'll attempt to fly. He starts running, around and around in a small but perfect circle. His head could be connected to a pole in the center, and like one in a herd of large breed animals, he leads himself round and round, his head tilted to the right, his body leaning inward at the shoulders, with only his smile an indication that he is satisfied with these stultifying movements. The words continue to come.

"Ahh! The Lord takes HOLD of me!" And his foot stomps. "YES! YES!" With each word that pours from him, his foot lands on the floor.

His arms shoot up then, and he waves heavenward. His eyes follow, imploring his whole spirit to come along. One senses that he doesn't wish to be there, spiritually or physically. There is also a sense that he must reach them all—reach in, take their souls, so that later he can offer them up to his god.

"I'm going on up, y'all," he says simply. "I'm going." He looks to the crowd, even stretches out his hands—emphatically, silently asking who will go with him.

"I'm going." He almost sings the words.

But who could or would believe it. There he is, you see, still there—still lifting his arms, still reaching, still promising. His voice, though ringing out clearly, begins to fade a little.

"I'm going, y'all." Softer.

"I'm going." A whisper. As his body turns round, with his back to his audience, he bends into a squat and stays there, pleading softly for someone to go with him.

There is a woman who sits on the left front pew of the crowded church. This is the first time she has come to River of Jordan Baptist Church. Yet, she appears quite comfortable sitting there. She has taken her slightly whimpering baby from her shoulder and placed it in the cup of her left arm, at her sizeable chest. Unbuttoning the two buttons that withhold her bosom—which has, to this point in time, adhered to all restraints—she reaches beneath her left breast and places it outside her bra.

This action helps her maintain the image of a not so well-dressed woman. Her look says she is tired. Her dark, almost chocolate face has no apparent age, though the puffy fullness of her expression suggests she is well into middle age. Her breasts still sit up like soldiers, ready to do battle, weapons pointing the way. They could be on a mission.

She has a rich brightness about her—what these colored folks call bright, at least—which means she knows something the rest of the world does not. Her dress is uncommonly gray, which adds to her average look. One is reminded of a not-yet-blooming rose against the cold, dark ground. Her short-sleeved dress is of some cheap, natural blend, worn so thin that her white underclothing is slightly visible from close up.

This visitor to the church does not smile. Her eyes never leave the preacher, as though she, too, is struck, or even bound by the levity of his words. One would think she is connected to the man in the pulpit somehow. Her eyes say she is interested in every movement he makes. As she sits there, with the one breast sitting on the outside of her dress, waiting for the baby to find its nipple, the preacher becomes aware that he is no longer the center of attention, that his words are falling nimbly upon closeted ears.

With curly fine black hair, the baby moves its already sucking lips in search of the nipple that everyone in the front of the church can readily see. The dark brown earthy color of the nipple matches that of the baby's lips, and when they meet, one will surely supplant the other, and the overall scene will not change. The color will still be there, like mud that won't cake, its richness making the men who sit in the Men's Corner want to take the baby's place. Nourishment like from above. And when the baby's lips finally steal home, having honed in on their target, perhaps by sense, perhaps by smell, perhaps by the sheer habit of doing so, one can almost feel men's souls being questioned. Something down below stirs—something that cannot be undone.

They allow their desires to wander, their hearts to fawn over a childhood memory, lost until that very moment. And though their eyes leave the woman—for they must—the men's attention remains there with the baby.

But the preacher, he is there, now still and motionless. He smiles upon the scene as though it is familiar to him and he has a duty to welcome it.

"Ahh," he says. "The Lord, God, said smite up your enemy but love him, too. Don't come undone my people!" He stands fully upright for the first time since he started yelling his praises and admonitions. His look is now defiant.

"Without further ado," he says and begins to jump up and down, with his large body coming down on the platform, the sound like a boulder hitting the ground. One can almost feel the pool's water waken and start to move.

The women in the Women's Corner sit up in their seats, move their purses to the other side of their bodies and then back again, and cease from saying "Amen." Their eyes begin to speak, leaving everyone around them to know that without a doubt, all is not well. One particular woman, who is old like cellar wine, sits in a wheelchair, with one leg propped up and the other dangling to the floor. She tries in vain to release the latch that keeps her chair from moving. Her look is beseeching.

A glance at the Men's Corner, and all seems well. The men sit raptly, hanging on to the preacher's words. Ganging up on him, they yell, "Say it, brother." Their words almost drown out the man in the pulpit. He is prodded on. Impelled to act. The jumping continues.

"I'm gonna walk on, chill-dren," he says. "No matter what. I'm gonna let the Lord use ME! USE ME, LORD! USE ME, LORD!" With every word he is a singing, jumping stone upon the surface.

Until, his last jump. The preacher man goes higher than anyone has seen a real live man jump before. His toes almost reach the top of the altar. His arms, clad in a black robe with white trim, hang from his side like the wings of a dead bird. He has a smile on his face that appears centrifugally forced into his teeth, which, though they remain closed, take on the appearance of being quite open and moving. His look says that life and death have converged.

When he comes down for the last time, hard upon the old and overused surface of the platform—the one that covers a baptizing pool below it, almost six feet deep at the preacher's end—the man in the pulpit splits the waiting boards into pieces and sinks into the dark, cold water that is now brightened by the light of day.

The splash is minimal. His submersion is like a diver's smooth, perfect entrance. None of the women in their corner, all of them dressed in white dresses and pretty matching shoes, are wetted.

But down to the right, just off from the pulpit, a piece of splintered board has flown through the air and landed in the chest of a young man sitting on the front pew, just across from the woman nursing her baby. This young man, whose name is Donnie—the only other visitor at River of Jordan Baptist Church on this day—has come seeking to mend the waywardness of his steps upon this earth. He has tumbled forward and is lying face down on the floor of the hushed and stunned church.

The preacher does not come up from the water. It is as though his body has sunk into a void, to a depth from which he cannot return.

Years later, the congregation, after much speculation, will conclude that the preacher man didn't want to come up again, that he knew all along he wasn't needed, not here in this world. They will surmise that the young man's death was the result of having done too much living in too short a time. The woman nursing her baby will not come through the church doors again, for shortly after church service that day, word flies through the neighboring community and kindly tells her that some people shouldn't bother being seen in their church, and she is one of those people.

Marguerite– 1985

She looks to her door just as a middle-aged woman begins to knock. It is a blustery spring day, as though Mother Nature is angry and hasn't had a chance to finish with winter.

Marguerite, at the lasting age of 82, has a son who has lived with her since his birth some twenty-five years since. The only other relative is a daughter who has been lost from her since shortly after her birth.

A typical response: They lived in a one-room shack in the back woods of Louisiana, and she beat the boy mercilessly because as a child, she, herself, had been beaten, or because she had been left suddenly by a man whom she loved more than life itself, or because she simply couldn't stand the sight of the boy and welcomed every opportunity to show her disdain for him. But, this can't be true, can it?

Which ending shall we use? Will any of them suffice?

End with her story.

This old woman has lived her life, much of it with her son, whom she has loved and protected and cherished, especially since her only other child, a daughter, was stolen from her as a baby many years before. The woman and the young man live in a small, three-room house in City of Orphans, Louisiana. She walks the roads, night or day, still looking for the child, knowing that her dying comes closer with every breath that she takes. She cooks bread pudding with juicy raisins in it for anyone who'll ask her, and she lies softly upon a worn-out caseless pillow when her head finally seeks slumber. She was once a practicing doctor—for that is what people called her—performing small services, but mostly healing women who had no use for a man and men who loved women the wrong way. No herbs and spells or any of that shit. She placed one hand upon the sickly person's forehead and allowed it to stay there until her work was done. Women and men got up from her dirty gray sofa and walked away without looking back. Some said she was giving up herself to those people, just letting her insides float out through her hands. Some said that's where her strength had gone, the little strength she had left after she lost her daughter. Some said she had been a fool, having to take care of that boy and all those wayward people as well.

Marguerite never invited people to her door, so it stood to reason that she never invited them in as well. But when this particular woman knocked at her door, Marguerite paid attention. Sitting with her legs partly open, so that her dress hung down in a crevice between her legs, she waited for the special visitor to enter.

The woman turned the door's handle and came up the two steps that led into the house. As the door opened and she saw Marguerite sitting in the small, half-lit room, watching her enter her home without permission, the woman trembled. Marguerite could feel her do so.

"Over there by the heater," her eyes told the woman.

To herself, Marguerite said: She's a fine something. Skin bright like lightning at night. Look at those eyes though; who done beat her heart out? Oh, dear God.

If her tears had not all dried up, Marguerite thought that she would cry for sure, so sad was she for humanity, but mostly herself.

Something was beginning to pull deeply at her heart.

They stared at each other at first. Marguerite knew why the woman was there, but she wasn't likely to tell her that.

The woman grew tired of the stillness between them.

"My name is Rachel," she said. Her voice was kind but clear and strong, and her face still youthful, though she was forty years old. She wore boots that ran up half her calves, just visible beneath a blue jean dress with a matching short coat. She crossed her legs at the ankles and her arms around her breasts and sat back on the sofa.

Marguerite's eyes were like dirty pools of water to Rachel. Suddenly, it didn't seem to matter how exact her words should be.

"I feel like I been traveling so long to get here, to see you. So many years. I don't know, I mean, I'm not sure how I knew to come. I just knew you could help me. Maybe I remember my mother and father talking about you in that roundabout way they did. I'm not sure they'd want me to come. My mother died some years ago, and my father just lost the will to live after she passed away. You know how people can become attached to others, so easily, and not let go..." As her voice trailed off, she looked down at her hands, now sitting awkwardly in her lap. She looked as though she would pray. She waited, this time for Marguerite to speak.

But nothing came. Marguerite was now screaming inside, trying to figure out what she would do. She sat back in an old rocker. The only sound outside Marguerite's head was the wee crinkling of paper each time the rocker came down on a piece of discarded gum wrapper.

Rachel thought the old woman was studying her in some way, as though she were reading each and every line on her face.

Just when Rachel was about to give up and attempt to make conversation, again, Marguerite stopped the rocker, pushed herself up from the seat, and moved slowly over to Rachel. When she reached her, Marguerite wanted to pull the woman up into her arms and keep her there forever, but instead she placed both her wrinkled, chocolate hands on the younger woman's forehead.

The women remained in that position for a few moments—Rachel sitting with her head erect and Marguerite standing before her. Marguerite's hands gently circled and soothed the top of Rachel's head.

Marguerite thought she would tell her daughter everything, right then, but knew the words would not come, not the way she wanted them to come. Instead, she began to speak freely about things Rachel might understand.

"All I can do is tell you about my own troubles. I believe that's what you ought to hear. All my life, I just wanted to be understood. But nobody did. I loved a man once, long ago, but he brought me nothing but pain. He may as well been the true meaning of sorrow. Since then, everybody saw me different than I saw myself, and not only that, they didn't care to get to know me. Not even Porter. He was Reverend Porter to most people. He turned out to be as bad as most preachers are good. Crazy enough, he had the idea he was supposed to save me, and part of me believed he could. He came here one day—just showed up out of the blue. He said he had come to claim my soul for the Lord and to send away the Devil. He was upset that he never saw me in church, said it was a sin to just ignore the Lord completely. He said just because my daughter had been stolen from me, that was no reason to give up on God. But I wasn't hearing him then. I was surviving on my own, without the Lord's help and Porter's too. I had a steady stream of people coming to my door, bringing me money, bringing me baskets of grocery, bringing me just about anything I could ask for. They even brought me this sofa you sitting on now. People brought me things because they knew I had the healing in my hands. The power just came up on me one day, after I lost my daughter. It's like she was working through me. I tried to tell Porter that I had both our strength—my daughter's and mine's, I mean—that the healing was God giving me something back for what he had taken from me. I sure didn't come by it on my own. But Porter wasn't listening to me, no more than I was listening to him.

"He came once or twice a week for a long time. He was still a good man then. He'd sit there by the heater and warm his heavy hands and just talk and talk. Every time he come, he had a different story but the same message: I needed to be in church like most everybody else.

"Then one day, he come like usual, but something was different. It's like he had turned into someone else. He had a strange look in his eyes, and I knew he had discovered a new way to hell. He was still talking his religion though. He told me he had talked to Abraham, and that Abraham surely knew the right path. He said I needed another child, that this child would cleanse me and save me. He said he knew I would bring that child to the Lord and bring myself, too. I'm gon' tell you right now, Rachel, I didn't know what the man was talking about. I was in my mid-fifties then and had long since give up on any more babies. I told Porter that he was talking nonsense, that he might better leave. I mean, I knew he was a man of God and all, but I didn't take to nobody coming in my house talking crazy.

"Then he turned on me. He throwed hisself on top of me. I struggled, but it wasn't no use. He was a big, big man. That's why he claimed so much respect, I always thought. A big man walking is hard to deny.

"After he was finished, he left, but before he walked out this house for the last time, he told me that God was going to use me, that I was going to be an instrument for the Lord, even if I didn't know it. Truer words ain't never been spoken. I had my baby. It was a boy; I named him Dominion, hoping he'd have his own place in life. I took him to church, just like Porter said I would. I showed up that day, dressed in as good a clothes as I had, and I sit me down right there on the front pew of his church. The moment he saw me, Porter started struttin' and a preenin'. He was getting around in that pulpit like he was top rooster in a fight. I just looked at him, and he looked at me. He may as well 'a saved the whole world, he was so happy to see me.

"Then he saw me nursing my baby, right there, on the front pew for everybody to see. I wasn't ashamed, but he sure was. I guess it was too much for him. I could see the spirit was about to drain out of him. I saw the end coming. It was staring me in the face—anybody really, if they was looking, could see it. He wasn't long for this world, and I believe he knew it."

Marguerite thought of Rachel then, and she thought about what she would say next.

Finally: "It was a shame that young man had to go with him, but you got to listen to me, child, it was his time to go. It had to be. When that splinter of a board came down in his chest, it was God speaking. It was final. I don't believe the great spirit, or God, or whoever you call him, takes us before our time. You got to know, it was his time."

Rachel gently pushed the old woman's hands away from her forehead.

Marguerite sat next to her on the worn sofa, still suppressing the need to throw her arms around her daughter, a daughter who still had no idea that Marguerite was her true mother.

They sat for a few minutes in the half darkness of the room without saying a word.

Until the door of the small house opened and Marguerite's son walked in. The house made a sucking noise as the door closed, and once again, they were all shut up.

The young man didn't know what to do. He hadn't seen his mother with a visitor in some years. He ceased his progress and waited at the door.

"This my son, Dominion," Marguerite said, to Rachel, almost imperceptibly.

Rachel, upon seeing the young man for the first time, wished to speak but could not. Something was knocking around in her heart now. She couldn't take her eyes away from him; she felt as if she were seeing Donnie all over again. She felt her body respond, almost like it had that day when Donnie had kissed her. This man's face, too, had that tired, used look about it. She didn't ask how this could be, how this young man, this replica of a man she had loved so many years before, could be standing before her now. She wanted to say something, if only to hear him speak in return. The only thing she could think to say, she said without pause: "I guess I should go, and get out of y'all's way."

Rachel set her feet to leave, even though she could feel there was something left to be said—as if someone was speaking to her, telling her to listen.

It was Marguerite's inner voice crying out, "Welcome home, daughter. Please don't go."

Rachel pushed the feeling aside. One step, then another. Just get up and you'll be able to walk away from here.

As she came to where Dominion was standing, she reached up to him—for he was a big man like his father Porter and his half-brother Donnie. She kissed him on his right cheek. A blessing. That is what it felt like to both of them.

Rachel then opened the door and stepped outside. The early evening air greeted her; it was too warm, and yet, she embraced it.

Marguerite watched from the window and saw Rachel's hair brush the back of her shoulders as she walked. Was Marguerite really going to let her child just move down the path and get in her car and drive away? With more sorrow than she had known in a long time, she forced herself to turn from the window. What could she do? What could she say now, all these years later? She looked to the old rocker as though it would save her.

Rachel's steps grew lighter, but old Marguerite's were heavier than they had ever been.

Salvia, Salvia

The guards brought him the food he liked without hesitation; he did not appear to miss his freedom; his noble body, full to almost bursting with all he needed, also seemed to carry freedom with it; this freedom seemed to reside somewhere in his jaws, and the joy of life burned so fiercely in his throat that it was not easy for the onlookers to bear it. But they steeled themselves, surged around the cage, and wanted never to leave it.

—From "The Hunger Artist," by Franz Kafka

salvia/sage: any of a large and widely distributed genus (Salvia) of herbs and shrubs of the mint family having a 2-lipped open calyx and two anthers; esp: one with scarlet flowers.

Salvia, Salvia, they called to her—old, contemptuous but right and sturdy women, that is. They had always known her, from when she was a baby. What you crying for? Got no Mama to lay your sleepy head on? No Papa to stroke your enormous little back? You'll be raised by the Wind. When He isn't fighting with old Thunder, that is.

She was a large mantle of a woman, with shelves to place all of her attributes on, so many they were. She was the second seed of humanity, and only because the first seed had already been planted and gathered—a true harvest, but not like her season. They said, She'll die long before news of her birth, and then she'll be reborn again. You know, like people who stand up in church and say they've been saved. It's only in that brief, obtrusive moment that everyone understands just how lost those persons had been.

But specifics…she had plenty.

Ooooh, weeeehe! One teeny voice in a room full of pretty little black girls, and a few tenacious boys. They are all black now, long before they became their other colors.

Ooooh, weeehe! Again, obstinately, but this time the student waits for the middle-aged teacher with her longstanding back to the class to turn and come with her blessing.

What your head all up about now, Petunia? The teacher can't simply ask the question; her presence at the girl's desk must remain long enough to satisfy the disruption.

The small child is used to the myopic rapport that she has with the teacher; she revels in that tiny ray of cultured attention.

She hands off her bit of information: Salvia was moving in her seat, Ma'am.

Of course the teacher must look the oddity's way. When she does, she won't find even a twitch or twitter from the overgrown and awkward girl sitting at the end of the first row of desks, her back forced to remain as straight and regal as the sun shining. Because she cannot fit into any of the miniature desks, she must sit in a solid wooden chair that, when it moves, makes the sound of two doors falling into each other. She holds her books and her paper tablet in her hands—all of this rests in the uncommonly long slant of her lap.

The teacher stares with eyes that have been too tested to wonder. Only the girl's head turns and faces the doubt and pity of her latest accuser. Her look briefly bounces off those other children's heads, for they've turned from her; they've suddenly grown tired of chastising her and have moved with their thoughts, and so very far away. She and the flowery acrid student do brief battle, with a smirk and a raised eyebrow or two, until the teacher comes back to Salvia, raps her on both hands with a thin and thorny limb which she has brought into class with her that very morning, and for this very purpose.

Salvia winces once before the first lick stains the back of her hand, and she does not move again. She steadies herself, chair and all, and becomes one mass of senseless dedication to their order. Over and over, they turn their eyes to set upon her, waiting for the mistake, the one move that will further limit her existence. Their thoughts wander away from her, but they always come back. These other children think that one day they will not be able to walk up to her and lay small, intruding fingers on her shoulders—shoulders too old and too well-made to be hers. They think of the length of her, how the backs of her legs lean so heavily on the chair, and how far those legs reach past her seat. She must cross them underneath her chair because they cannot fit under another child's desk. They all fear and pity her equally and instinctively; something like common sense tells them that she is still growing.

As the years pass and she's gotten tired of hearing that she's sprouted up too fast, that she was kept in the planter too long, that she's little more than a weed in transition—or in the plain talk of her former classmates: You's too old and way too big to be in that same class, girl—she makes the only choice she will make for her short lifetime. Instead of being the watched, the prodded, the seen, and the spectacled, she becomes the only one who can truly see herself.

Upon entering the class on that first day of that long and sightful year, in that same class, Salvia places her stiff and stifling chair—which has become worn over the years from her sitting, breathing form—against the wall, next to the lone window on the sunny side of the small room. By now, the teacher fears Salvia's breaking stare and dares not question her. When the back of her head finds rest upon the wall, she feels a nimble, generous radiance massage the back of her shoulders. She leans into this one small pleasure; it may as well be a welcoming kiss from strangers. Bonding with nature so unassailably, she begins to think she will become someone else, soon.

Every day, she sits in the classroom and sees the little people who share her world. Her eyes slap against the sides of small half-washed faces and big ostrich-shaped ears and stumble across the tops of heads like airplanes without landing gears, for she has become so fascinated in watching them that she cannot stop. Her smile gorges on braids too fat and too short to run peaceably down little girls' necks. She flips laughter inside her head when she notices ringworms making their rounds in little boys' heads. She feels, in her just beginning to broaden heart, like the bigger person now, without ever thinking that she had always been.

Was it the sun all that time, sitting next to that window? The old, contemptuous but right and sturdy women asked, rhetorically, banally. They knew the answer. Her scarlet color came as she shuffled her way through puberty. Her face, her arms, her abundant, winding body, all of it, even her shadow, became a hue of red most of them, other than the most elderly, had never seen. Some said Old Wind, her father now, had gone down, around, and back from Africa to find that color, special for her. No, some others said, Just to those old clay slopes of Louisiana; y'all listen now. But it was just her time. She'll be starting to blossom, soon, they agreed.

By then, she had become a flowing definition of the word beautiful. All of her spread out resplendently upon her journey to here and there. Her arms were like the floating fans of large flora; her lithe, supple body soared upon the admirer's senses; her eyes gathered and gazed gratuitously from beneath lids that opened at their ease. When she walked, or strutted herself down the very hill that kept her safe and storaged away, those same boys who had once ridiculed and teased her into her other world, now, as teenagers, noticed her as she went away from them. They could never see all of her fine and graceful figure—only her backside, her bottom working one side before it began working the other side. These were hips that were too young and too old to behave so, and yet they did.

That is when the older boys from the neighborhood would attempt to climb the steep, aggravating hill to her house—trudging ever upward, their bodies working as though they were sails against a windward tide. It was a short but thorough hill. And they were on stairs taking them nowhere they needed to be.

And when some one of those boys would make it to her bedroom door or her window, which always lay open and waiting, that boy always came with something eager and falling off the bones like the tenderness of young rib meat. And he would offer it to her before he left and went emboldenedly and assuredly down the hill again, as though he'd returned from death's sordid camp with survivors.

As the boys became the youngest of men, they continued to come to her, as best they could. In the darkness of sassy-spring evenings, they came to her. And she sat with her backside hanging out the windowsill, leaving a small glare of moonlight to shoot past her and settle on the thin, not so tender gifts of youth. The moonlight would then molest their backs and their dark brown thighs, as their arms angrily dropped shadows, and pants and shirts, tossing away encumbrances to what they knew to be lovemaking—clothes they would later search for in the softer, more silent darkness of their spent night.

She watched them. Their heads were always down at first. Heads that she would know even if her eyes were taken away from her. Those same tops of skulls and craniums from her youthful years when she laughed her frightened thoughts away from tears—when she feared she would never be one of them; when they looked at her and only saw her blackness, though, oddly enough, they could not feel that same blackness sifting through her as she grew older and found her own contempt of them. When she grew tired of their intrusions, she simply sent them all away.

Those had been her youthful, growing-into-a-woman years. Don't leave me. Some said she began to cry these very words to Father Wind. And what about Nights' followers of still but not satisfied dreams? or maddening and deceiving Luck leaving home again? or budding, incipient Life, bursting to come out of her?

Who whittles away destiny so carelessly, they said. Get up girl, and be about your father's business. To some, this meant, Go to church; save yourself before it's too late. To everyone else, this meant, We know nothing about you. Come on, now. Let us get to know you.

But how easily could she find herself where she had never been? Even if she attempted the journey, only small pieces of her would have come along, and then those sacred, frightened to death pieces would say, Get back, and stay away! to every new and brave thing she had sought to become. She knew this like she knew nothing that had ever presented before her—so she stayed at home.

This is when the passersby, upon moving slowly and intentionally along the base of the hill of her house, like cows and horses on their way to stables, would have to stop and mull over the noises that they heard coming from the defiant, yet shadowy house above. None of them knew, at first, that these were the sounds of her footsteps coarsely roaming across her gigantic floors. The listeners talked amongst themselves, trying to decipher the sonorities of her world. Some thought the clamor was complicitous like men moving chifferobes from an ex-lover's bedroom. It's just old Thunder, the older, wiser folk said. Some swore there were massive bombs being set off in a smaller world next door.

Those same young men who had come to her so many years before, now brought their families to stop on their way to church and to stand and listen, their eyes darting softly from father, mother, children, their thoughts aglee and transparent, hoping to catch a sighting of the woman who had stored herself away. And soon there would be crowds of others, mostly families but some single folk with nothing better to do—and there they'd stand in a virtual commonality of awe.

No one knew why they came, or why they stayed, sometimes days even, listening to her move about that obviously empty place, so high on the hill, so removed from them, so alien the reasons of her remaining there—they simply stood and listened, and eventually, it bothered not one of them that they could not see her. For somehow, they knew those magical sounds would be lost from them if she were suddenly to come down from that dwelling above and exist as one of them.

But, you know time always passes and people always transplant their old notions onto someone else—someone who doesn't care much about such things. It was then that knowing only the sounds of her became like the unbearable awkwardness of a neighbor's overused but not yet broken arguments. The harrumphing of her heels became too lazy and too tired as they scraped across what must have been sinking, fading floorboards. Bluntly: the sense of it just didn't ring so faithfully any more. People began to wonder how she could remain in that house, without even the sun's nectar to feed her. The children had long grown bored, and as their parents made motions to slow or to stop for a quick listen, the children would push forward, or scatter one by one seeking out each other's more gratifying presence. These children—as children are likely to be—were the first to take their thoughts on away from her.

To one who likes to communicate, silence is unbearable—it causes people to talk, to explicate life as best they know how; and this they learned to do for her. She still patterns her life on the outside edges of dreams, some said. The more learned said, That house is like a cell that needlessly encases animals too old or too brittle to survive. They all finally declared, She'll be worshipping the ground or some other such nonsense in a minute. They were all upturned in their thoughts, bothered by the fact that she had shut herself off from them, without even a miniscule, momentary movement in their direction.

But for people who truly want to know something, they know how to ask, and in just the right way. And besides, the way the world was starting to look, most of them were getting afraid of life's repercussions. Every young or old thing growing had begun to give in to a sadness that felt like weeds intruding, and they were all becoming stiff and close to breaking. You know that kind of brownness that floors the earth, leaving the vibrant colors to chase at their own tails? Well, it went and stayed wherever it pleased. They were all becoming stickly, sickly things, like sliced thorns, and there was no protection from each other.

So, they went about with new resolutions. Heeyyy, oohhh? they called up to her one day. Salvia, Salvia? No one expected to get a clear answer; they would have been satisfied with an old harrumphing or thumpumpbadum from the old days when she'd first locked herself away—any real and vibrant movement, any sound that decided to join them there on the pavement would be welcomed. Their heads twitched about like people who had been out in the garden and had gotten bitten by ants or gnats that they could barely see. Many of them thought about abandoning the mission—Whose bright idea was this? they thought about saying. Others thought of gathering their daffodiling children, who skirted about in the noon sun as though the assembled occasion was an opportunity to show themselves off. Yes, thoughts were going around, bouncing from one person then finding another.

Of course they were surprised when she did, in one heavy moment, bring her bountiful head to droop out the fronthouse windowsill. She stood there waiting for someone to speak again. She couldn't tell them that she had grown tired and fearful of her own large self and that she was now repulsed by the thought of being alone. Or that she had just begun to scream off a small plea for help when she heard their call. Or that their clattering voices actually sprung upon the darkness that was beginning to engulf her entire being, frightening what was left of her into a new direction of light.

That's all it took. It all recommenced with her whisper to Life's mother to let her bloom again. She wasn't a flower, like all the others. She accepted the small truth and waved her small handkerchief to the Sky. It was a sign that few of them noticed.

She stepped first one then the other of her long, fatted legs down the hill until both stayed upon the grassy pavement of the roadway. She stood there all bubbling over in her own silent laughter. And although she was only a watered version of her most scarletted self, no one knew of it. Oh, she's ripe, they said. And not all rough and edgy. Girl, this child was stepping, they later said. Ah, the richness of her new skin, just short of velvet in softness. She gleamed at them, without smiling. She bore down into their cores with joyousness.

And although none of them had ever heard her speak, even her name, before, she now pursed her lips as if to sing. She puffed up her cords so that they could reach Father Wind carrying Himself and many others miles and miles away.

"I, I, I, I, I, I, I, I know I been changed. I, I, I, I, I, I, I, I, I know I been changed. I, I, I, I, I, I, I know I been changed…somebody, like angels maybe, somebody signed my name."

Oh, Lord, blaspheme, some of the people cried. That sounds like the old Negro spiritual she mumbling about. But they were too late with their objections, she had gone on.

"Stepped in the water, and the water was sooooo cold, y'all. Look like it chilled my big old body, but didn't dare chase my soul. Somebody, somebody, y'all, somebody signed my name."

Lord, Lord, the old, contemptuous but right and sturdy women were called on to say. But they knew her. Let her go, now, they said. Don't go messing with His business. From that moment on, everyone listened and she became the only voice they heard.

She went on and on: "Sometimes I'm up, and sometimes I'm down; sometimes, I'm level to the ground; oh yeah, these somebody's, these somebody's, y'all, they called my name."

Before they knew it, she had stepped over a few of the youngsters and even some elders, so did she tower above them. Her wide legs were as red as that sea over in Africa.

Collection

Myths of Cotton

Even in the 1960s, in the small hamlets of Louisiana, men and women worked long and hard in the fields of cotton—sometimes, the women with babies on their hips and toddlers following close behind. Altogether, they were a giant on the field, a pushing bulk of dark bodies weaving through the dirty white cotton. They didn't do it because they were being forced by other men who did not want to labor; they did it because they were small farmers, working their own land, because the only way to bring in the crop was by hand. This money would keep their bellies full for a good portion of the year.

Boy Gabriel and his brother Peter understood how and why land was reserved for cotton; Boy was sixteen and his brother fourteen. They had taken over what their grandfather left behind. The grandfather had taught them well: how to get up early before the sun came looking too hard. The grandfather put Boy behind a mule when he was only twelve. The scene remained fresh in Boy's mind. He stood there with the long straps hanging across his thin shoulders, his fingers laced between the straps and the handles of the plow, his feet planted solid in the rich brown topsoil. "Get up!" his grandfather had then shouted to the mule, and the animal had taken off, almost like a spasm had shot through it and forced the animal to action. Boy had tried to keep up. His feet slid against the earth—he may as well have had skis on—and he was being pulled through the snow. The plow twisted and tried to lie down instead of remaining straight, and Boy struggled to keep it upright. The row that Boy was plowing was as crooked as his grandfather's previous rows were straight.

"Whoa," his grandfather had finally said, releasing Boy from his torture. His grandfather then said nothing. He took the reins from Boy, stood in his place, straightened the plow, and began to move forward. "Come on, now, Jake!" he said to the mule. "Get up, now!"

A funny thing happened after that first attempt: Boy watched his grandfather more closely. He saw the way his grandfather commanded the mule to go and to stop, the way his grandfather stood with his back straight but able to bend when he needed, how the plow needed a man's guidance to remain upright as it cut through the always-difficult earth. Boy couldn't remember if it was then days or weeks later before his grandfather put him behind the plow again. The important thing was that Boy took to the plow like his grandfather wanted, like he had planned.

Within three months, his grandfather was gone. Boy recalled that his grandfather's sickness had come like rude people who visited but never wanted to leave their home, at least not until they'd eaten up all the tea cakes and drunk up all the buttermilk. After his grandfather had taken to his bed, he never got up again. Death then seemed fickle. It was his grandfather, trying to hold on—perhaps he knew how much his old wife and two young grandsons needed him.

Every year since their grandfather's death, Boy and his younger brother had planted a cotton crop. Somewhere along the way, Boy had also grown up sturdy and upright; his grandfather might have said Boy was blessed by the will of the plow. Boy passed on to his brother what his grandfather taught him, but it was only Boy Gabriel who had truly learned to plow.

Every year when cotton picking time came around, it was Boy and his brother Peter, alongside their grandmother, who made their way out to the fields. They bent their backs low and reached out with a sweeping motion of their hands, grabbing at the bushes of cotton, pulling until the pods were empty and dark.

Sweet Stuff Andy

Generally, I like it when a man calls me one of those saccharine names like Honey or Sugar; it always gives me the impression that the man in question would like to eat me up—like he's got a hungering jones for me. And when is that a bad thing, right? It reminds me of this guy named Andy. I called him Sweet Stuff 'cause that's what he dealt in: sweet comments flowed from his lips right into my ears. Andy used to work at one of those companies that hire the mentally challenged, which means Andy was "kinda whack," as the kids used to say. Back when I was growing up we called people like Andy "retarded," or "slow," or simply, "He ain't right." Today, we think better of others. Me, I think we all got a few challenges to overcome, right? So, the work at this small packing company was simple enough—monotonous, and it only required a little dedication from the people who worked there.

I was a woman truck driver back then; let me tell you, I knew how to get a rig down the road. When I pulled into the little company where Andy worked, I would park my truck out by the dock and walk around to the front of the building. The boss's secretary doubled as the shipping/receiving clerk, and she would beep me in. As soon as I walked in the door, Andy would come running from the lunchroom or from somewhere in the warehouse. It was kinda weird, actually—I often wondered if the man could smell my presence, like I was giving off some kind of perfume that only he could detect. Later, I realized that Andy operated on a clocklike existence—things like schedules and receiving times and appointments not only fascinated the hell out of him, they made his life bearable. They brought order to the chaos that must have gone on inside his head.

"Good morning," Andy would say to me, smiling. He had this way of talking with his entire body getting in on the conversation. His arms flapped uncontrollably, which twisted his torso and jerked his knees up as he walked, like a stud prancing.

"Good morning, Andy," I would say, and darn if I would not smile also because he had that effect on me. Perhaps I knew what was coming and my heart was beginning its little dance.

"Ah, Ms. Willow," he would say, just getting warmed up with his compliments. "You sure look sweet today."

"Do I, Andy?" I would say—it was the same reply every time, for it must be. Andy inspired nothing less.

"Oh, yes, ma'am, you sweeter than lemon ice box pie today." He always had to qualify my supposed sweetness on that day, leaving tomorrow or the next visit open to new possibilities of his charm. In all the time I knew Andy (which was about a year), it was never the same dessert twice. If I was chocolate pudding one day, the next day I was peach cobbler. I was pralines and cream ice cream, strawberry shortcake, and Bluebell vanilla ice cream. The compliments seemed endless.

One day I came from the bathroom to find Andy waiting for me. I knew something was off because, as I said, he didn't tolerate changes in his schedule. But that day, he had been acting all weird from the time I showed up. He had actually described me as mincemeat pie, which, when I heard him say it, I found strange. No one talked about mincemeat pie, probably not even people who liked to eat it. Was it even a dessert?

So, as I came out of the bathroom and tried to walk past Andy, he grabbed me by my arms, all stern like he was a father trying to correct his child. Let me say that Andy, although childlike in demeanor, was strong and possessed the physique of a middle-aged man. His hands on my arms felt like I had been tied down—a ship moored, or a tent anchored from the wind.

I tried to move away from him gracefully, not wanting to upset his gentle nature, but Andy held on. If anything, his hands clamped around my arms even tighter.

"Andy," I struggled to say. "What's going on, man?"

He looked into my eyes, and I saw that his real nature—that thing that makes a man a man—was coming through. It was evident that he intended to plant a kiss on me, somewhere, even if the kiss missed my lips and landed on my ears or upside my head, he was going to do it.

"No," I said. "Andy, I need to get by."

Still he said nothing. I could feel him drawing closer to me. Then it was me struggling, to extricate myself, to be on my way.

"My truck's ready," I said, thinking this might slip him back into reality.

"I aim to kiss you, Ms. Willow," he finally said. "I aim to kiss you right here."

"Oh, my," I said, even though I was already clear on his intentions. The words just fell out of me, the only escape available.

We stood like this for what seemed like an hour—with him shaking but managing to hold me still and submissive—until his lips did actually find mine. The roughness of his skin was surprising. The hair above his upper lip brushed against my nose, and I wanted to sneeze but the urge went away. There was no tongue trying to find its way into my mouth, but a bit of saliva did seep onto my own dry lips.

It must have lasted a few seconds, and when Andy pulled back, I could feel his hands soften and then release me. I expected that he would turn and leave me standing there, somewhat dumbfounded, me suddenly "slow" and "not quite right."

"Thank you, Ms. Willow," he said. "I knew you was sweet as pie, good juicy pecan pie with vanilla ice cream on top. Thank you, Ms. Willow."

Then he was gone. He sort of shook himself down the hall and then turned to go back in the warehouse where the other workers were sorting Mardi Gras beads and repackaging them.

I stood there for a few moments longer, still tasting Andy's kiss.

Alfre and Viola at the Clothes Hop

I come into the Laundromat the other day, and soon as I get my two loads of clothes in the machines, I go over and sit at one of the three tables they got in the place. Pretty soon I notice two women at the table next to me. Immediately I think they could be knockoff versions of the actors Alfre Woodard and Viola Davis—one even has a long, burnt red weave and is smoking on a cigarette. I see Alfre in that movie where she's an aspiring writer, strung out on heroin, and tries to sell her daughter to her drug pimp. I never remember the name of that movie.

So, in front of me, the Viola character is sitting across from the Alfre character and leans forward holding her head in her hands, making a low moaning sound. She's got a look on her face like she and Meryl Streep are facing off—I swear it's like she's living her own as well as someone else's hell. She's probably still wearing the same evening gown she had on the night before (actually, it ain't really a gown so much as it's an old dress, mostly for laying 'round the house in).

Alfre clears her throat in that way she's got. "Girl, you look like you still high," she says.

"Yeah, I didn't leave the party 'til three this morning," Viola returns. She drops her arms on the table, and using them as a pillow, her head falls.

"Excuse me?" Alfre says, dragging on the cigarette, and dragging her words out like she doesn't know how to stop. "I don't see no sense in it," she finally says, turning her head to look out the oversized window.

These words rouse Viola somewhat. She's on the defense now, owning her mistakes. "You know you can't get away once Bop get started with his stories."

"Okay," Alfre says, in that way she answers you with a word that sounds like she's asking a question. "What he talking 'bout now?" she asks.

"He had me laughing so hard."

"Girl, what?" Again, dragging that one last syllable to death.

"He said Chicken, you know, Letty's oldest, is in jail."

"What for this time?"

"Fool was walking by a white man's house when he saw one of them golf carts just sitting there, keys in the ignition, running, the whole thing. I guess the old man was just over in the bushes, pulling out some weeds. So Chicken hop on the cart and take off. He drive in to town, all up and down the streets, waving at people like he important or something." Viola says this.

"Girl, you is a lie," Alfre returns.

"On my people, I tell you. Bop said when the police finally caught up with the fool, he didn't even try to run. Just got out the cart, stood there laughing and grinning like he ain't going to jail." With that last part, Viola sits up fully, like she's actually present for this conversation now. Those sleepy-to-alert eyes of hers look fully open.

"So what happen?" Alfre asks.

"I don't know, child. Pretty sure he still locked up."

The ladies then go quiet, like sitting in each other's company is good enough, and not awkward at all. I take the opportunity to slip away from my little made up movie and check my clothes, to see if they're ready for the dryer.

When I get back, Alfre is puffing on a new cigarette and Viola is talking a new story about Chicken and the time he got hit in the head with a wrench by his so-called girlfriend. I swear her eyes get bigger as she talks. Her dark skin glistens, even though it's clear she's tired and worn out from an extraordinary night of partying.

"You know what," Alfre says, "you better slow your ass down." Spoken like a wiser sister.

"You ain't got to tell me," Viola returns. "What I know about gettin' high?"

"You know how we get, girl," knockoff Alfre says. For the first time I notice the dress she's wearing; it's thin and worn out, too. The thin straps are about to fall down, off her shoulders. She is barefoot, as her shoes sit against the base of the table. She's got one elbow on the table and the other hand moving here and there, the cigarette smoke leaving a trail. I briefly wonder who comes to the Laundromat dressed like this.

Some other woman moseys over to their table; she sorta look like the chick that plays in practically every black movie ever made—Loretta Devine. Her voice is all high and singsongy and in moments raggy, like she's the one chain smoking. "Y'all didn't hear about Chicken, huh?"

Alfre and Viola look at her all strange. I can tell they think she's intruding, taking up their space.

"I heard y'all talking about him, thought you might not know."

"Know what?" Alfre says, still dragging words.

"Chicken dead," Loretta says.

Alfre clears her throat.

"But," Viola says, "he in jail." She is clearly at a loss for words. Simply incredulous.

"He was," Loretta informs them. "But you know Chicken, can't keep him still long."

"Well, you gonna tell us what happened?" Alfre snaps. She's upset at this woman for dropping this impertinent news on her and Viola.

"I hear tell, the man dropped the charges, so they had to let Chicken out. He was walking down the street early this morning and somebody shot him. They don't know who did it."

"Of course they don't," Alfre says. "Who know anything these days?" She throws her head to the side. "People," she says. "What's wrong with folks? They're lucky I don't…"

Viola reaches over to her friend. "What we gonna do 'bout a world this crazy, huh?" They share a look; it's a look of understanding, one that says, "Yeah, girl, I'm with you on that." The both of them stare out the big windows, their eyes scanning the cars passing by on the street, as though they're looking for Chicken to be riding around in one of them.

"Thought y'all'd want to know," Loretta says, as she slinks away, back to a bundle of clothes that she hasn't even put in the washer yet.

"Remember when that girl from Mississippi was gonna marry him?" Alfre finally asks.

"Yeah," Viola says. "Back then we thought Chicken might make it."

"Okay?!" Alfre throws out. "I'm just saying."

Eventually, both women get up and start pulling their clothes from the jumbo washers. Alfre in her bare feet. Viola still moving slow, looking like her head's about to explode.

White Faces at Funerals

Robbie came to my older brother's funeral. He sat up front with the family, like he was truly one of us, or perhaps it was because he wanted everyone else to know he was there, saying goodbye to his friend. He was dressed in sneakers and an old Polo shirt, totally inappropriate to black folks. He shoulda worn a black suit and a nice pair of shoes to pay proper respect. This is what people would say later, at the repast, after Robbie had come and gone. But I forgave him this small error in etiquette since I knew he and my brother had been friends, close to being brothers, carousing through the nights, picking up dirty women, drinking cheap beer, making trouble where they could—basically being not-so-careful with their lives.

When the funeral was over and we had gone to the cemetery, a few brave souls walked up to me and other family members and asked outright, "Who that white boy?" and "How he related to y'all?" I wanted to mockingly say, "That white boy over there? He's our brother," but thought better of it. You still couldn't exactly joke about things like that back in those days—I mean, we were still having marches and things. Not to mention this solemn occasion and us all up in the middle of laying my brother to his eternal rest. These odd people who were asking who Robbie was, they seemed satisfied with the truth: Robbie was missing his friend and wanted to be at the funeral. No one spoke of an apparent but unwritten rule in the deep South at the time: blacks and whites should remain separated, if not in their schools then definitely in their churches.

Actually, Robbie hadn't started anything special, or different enough for people to take notice. When my dad had died some years earlier, Mr. John, an old white man from the Parish, had come to my dad's funeral. Mr. John and my dad had gotten to know each other near the latter part of their lives. They often sat around, talking about the old days when whites and blacks did not mix nearly as well as they do nowadays.

"I always liked you," my dad had initially said to Mr. John, who had responded, "Yeah, I liked you, too."

From then on, they had met at the corner grocery where they had sat out front, on the stoop, gossiping about their particular business. To local bystanders, and those passing along the street, these two old men probably looked strange, but my dad and Mr. John got a kick out of it.

At my dad's funeral, Mr. John showed up. He sat way in back of the choir because all the pews were filled with the black faces of my dad's family and friends. The crowd was thick, heavy, and Mr. John stood out. He also stood up on my dad's behalf; he told us just how strange his relationship with my dad had not been. He talked about my dad as the quintessential friend, someone he had grown to depend on, like when Mr. John's wife died and the regular people stopped coming. He could always count on my dad to be sitting there on the stoop, waiting for a conversation. "Oh, we talked about the war," Mr. John said. "And we talked about life when we came home, about our women who were missing and the new women we met and then married. We talked about the weight our children had left on us, and we talked about hard work and cotton fields and about plowing mules." Mr. John's voice seemed to slide into a deeper, sadder realm as he spoke. We all knew that the things he was saying were true, that we could trust that Mr. John was going to miss my dad about as much as we would.

After we left the cemetery, where all the extended family and not-so-close friends had asked us, "Who is that white boy?" we made our way to the family home—where my dad had lived since he returned from the war many years before. Both my parents were gone, and now the oldest of our siblings, our brother, was gone as well. My brother had lived a rough and careless life, and he died from liver failure.

Perhaps this is why Robbie came back to the house with us after we left the cemetery. Perhaps he felt guilty for all the nights he and my brother had drunk so much that they sometimes couldn't even make it home. Or maybe this was a wakeup call, and he was seeing firsthand where his own life was headed. He stood around like the rest of us, holding plates filled with fried chicken and baked macaroni and red beans and rice, not to mention so many different kinds of homemade cakes and pies that we wondered how many days it would take to finish them.

Every once in a while, Robbie would take a bite of something, and his eyes would wander around the room. I noticed that most of the people had moved on and no longer cared about his sad white face amongst so many of our black ones.

Nina, Don't You Weep

There was a set of twins—Nina and Besina—who had grown to be middle-aged mothers and wives, and upstanding members of their small community. One day, Besina showed up at her sister's house, all sudden, like it was a true emergency. Besina walked in—and she did so as though she were the true owner of the house, as though she had every right to subsequently instruct and belittle the people who were living there.

Walking in the door, Besina found the usual disheveled house, for her sister was never overly concerned about the neatness of anything, particularly houses. She cleaned when it was necessary, not out of any sense of daily ritual. Nina was no doubt in the kitchen, for it was there that she felt most comfortable. With so many children in the family (eight eventually), it was also there that she was most needed. She always kept food on the table, three meals a day, meals that knocked the children and the husband's proverbial socks off.

So Besina made her way into the kitchen, sat down at the table, and made herself feel welcomed. "Made herself" because most of the children had long dreaded their aunt's visits—even Nina was generally irritated by these visits. Once, when Nina had gone into the hospital to birth yet another child, she ended up staying longer than expected because the baby was almost fourteen and a half pounds at birth and brought on obvious complications for Nina. Besina had come to the house then and told the children that they needed to "clean up," that if the house was cleaner, "maybe people wouldn't be getting sick so much." Never mind that their mother wasn't so much sick as she was near to bursting open, trying to give birth to a giant baby. The oldest of the children was thirteen then and she could almost appreciate her aunt's visit, but even she knew there was a time and place to stomp "some sense into people," and that time wasn't when their mother was away in the hospital.

Their aunt rallied the children to her cause though, telling them that "God could not dwell in an unclean house" and neither should they. She also told them that their mother would be happier if she came home to a clean home. It took a while, but the children cleaned every floor and washed every dish and every dirty piece of clothing and hung out the sheets and spreads on the clothes line, then left open all the windows in the house so only fresh air would come in. When the aunt finally left their house, many hours later, only after the day had completely spent itself, the children noted that the house was the cleanest it had ever been.

So, this particular day when Besina showed up like she had an emergency to deal with, she sat at the kitchen table and attempted to have "an edifying conversation" with her sister Nina—in this conversation Nina would be the listener and Besina would be the talker.

"Nina," her sister said.

"Yes, Sina," she answered. She kept moving around in the kitchen, her graceful body shifting here and there, dropping the first dumplings, stirring peas, checking on pies in the oven.

"People are talking." Besina shifted her own body then, not so much out of need as from not being embarrassed to have this conversation. She wanted to sit just right when she dropped this particular verbal bomb on her sister.

"'Bout what, Sina?"

"About you and Robert and these children smelling."

Nina moved back to the table then and addressed her sister face to face. She didn't believe in talking at people. She could look at a person and make them wish they were someplace else. Nina was cooking chicken pie that day, and she began to flatten another ball of dough before she cut it into two by three-inch rectangular dumplings. She continued doing this, but the sound the rolling pin made as she slapped it against the dough was unmistakable: she was pissed off. She was angrily ruminating over what her sister had said.

"Nina, did you hear me?" Besina asked.

"You know I heard you. I'm right across the table from you."

"Well, what you going to do? No need to get upset about me coming over here trying to help you keep these children clean."

"I ain't never had no problem keeping my children clean, and you know it."

After a moment of reflection, Besina said, "Well, maybe they talking about Robert. I see him in that same suit almost every Sunday. Are you having it cleaned at least?" Nina's husband had recently been trying to become a deacon, after many years of boozing and chasing women.

But Nina didn't think of herself as her husband's shield or conscience, and she told her sister, "Robert's a grown man and he wears what he wants to. You got a problem with that, you need to talk to him. He out there in the garage; I can call him."

This slowed Besina down, but after a few moments, she recharged: "It ain't right, that's all. He all up in church, before people; he ought to be clean. You know the Lord don't...."

"I know, Sina, the Lord don't dwell in no unclean place."

Nina kept rolling dumplings. No more words came from her. By then, she had given her sister the look that said she was done talking.

Besina got up from the table to leave, but before she made a step, her sister said, "Stay for supper? You know I can set another plate."

"No, thank you. I need to be getting home to make my own dinner."

"Alright, give me a call when you get home."

And with that Besina politely went on her way. But that night, Nina ran a tub of warm (almost too hot) water, with a couple of capfuls of Lysol, for every person in the house, starting with her husband. She did so because she knew there were roving eyes—some of them trying to trip her up and help her fall down life's stairway. And when the day was fully over, and she could finally lay her head on her pillow, she turned away from her husband and shed a couple of quiet, harsh tears.

Bayou Buoys

She saw a row of women gingerly passing a baby down through them. The baby was curled up and resembled a ham with booties. The baby had a sour look on its face. She waited for the baby to cry, or to demand in some way that the women handle it more delicately.

She witnessed the hundred or more people—local sheriffs, state troopers, agents, and just plain folks—many of them dressed in slicker overalls and rubber boots, threading their skiffs down the water roadways of the bayou. Dead cypress trees stood like pointy shepherds keeping watch over the throng of men and womenfolk ferrying through the muck. The flat-bottomed boats moved slowly over patches of thriving lilies and hyacinths. The day was cool and ashy in appearance—gray and white, with no greens to speak of—and it was hard to see where they were going.

The mother told the reporter, "They always was fine boys. I can remember them jumping off the bayou, swimming all day long if I let 'em. Seem like all I could see was they feet flying in the air."

The little lady reporter asked her, "You all weren't afraid of alligators and snakes and such living this far back?"

"No, not rightly," the mother said. "They could swim almost out the womb."

The reporter didn't ask what being good swimmers had to do with not being afraid.

The boys were now missing for almost three days. Their mother and all the men and women of the neighboring camps had searched the surrounding areas of Cochon Bayou. The state troopers and FBI had finally given up, or moved their search further out, but the local sheriffs were diligent in shifts, afraid to say the obvious: the boys were gone. The thing is, the mother hadn't given up yet, so none of the local folks felt right about giving up. When they went home and crawled into their beds, the last thing they could see was the mother's face, her lips speaking desperation, her eyes wide open with hope. "We'll get back out there first thing," she said, matter-of-factly, like it was a foregone action they would take. Her face followed them into their dreams.

The woman had gone into the general store; she needed to buy some khakis for the boys' new school year. "Both of them wore out last year's uniform," she said. The store clerk nodded, but did not offer an answer to the woman. The woman rummaged through all the stacks on the table. Her disheveling of the pants that the store clerk had only recently righted gave a messy appearance to the store.

The store clerk asked, "What size you need?" But she knew it was already too late.

How could she not cheer the woman on? Hope with all hope that the woman's life would not become a full-out tragedy? The reporter thought of a story she had read once about a woman named Mary, who, in the face of defeat, had stood defiantly and thrown up her middle finger to the world. Of course it took Mary a while to do this. She had spent the entire story with her head stuck up her ass, trying to avoid life's little delicate battles. The reporter had assumed that Mary would remain a static character, having changed little, and deserving none of her sympathy. So many people, she had thought, are just like Mary—stagnant, trying to play it safe when there is no safety net below them. Perhaps they know this, and this could be the reason why Mary refused to fly so high that any damage might be done. What a witless, poor life they must lead in the meantime, the reporter thought. As she watched this woman, so certain that her boys would be found, without a thread of doubt touching her tired, relentless body, the reporter could recognize something special in the woman. She recognized it as something she wanted for herself.

That night the baby had turned into a pig and some of the women stood off in a corner sharpening knives. The baby whined and squealed, its little voice growing in strength. She knew the baby would rage on, refusing their efforts to stop it from crying. They passed the baby around again. As it neared the end of the row of women, the woman woke up and could still hear the sound of knives grating against the stone heap.

The police boat sat tugging and thumping outside the woman's camp. Two men had gotten off and were standing on her gallery knocking. A bull frog hopped from an old can filled with grimy water and landed near the boat.

The men told her that some pieces of clothing had been found about two miles in, down one of the innermost swamp roads, and could she come take a look. The men were the local sheriff's deputies, better known as Hawk and Pup Dan.

She had slept in her clothes that night, sleep having arrested her before she could get undressed. She stepped into the flat-bottomed skiff and sat down on a shabby bench. She held on to the side of the boat, which coughed occasionally as it headed deeper into the rich blue waters. The woman wanted to smell the freshness of the morning; it was rare that she took such an extended ride into the bayou. She and the boys normally kept close to camp, except for those rare beautiful days when they journeyed into the swamps, searching out the fullest patches of blue irises, which bloomed only a precious few weeks. The boys always laughed at how the blooms peeked out from the tupelo trees. A smile almost came to the woman; she pushed it back into her face. She knew her children were still out there somewhere, and that's why she couldn't waste time remembering happier days or enjoying this incredible view. She would see the beauty God created some other day, when her boys were home.

Sitting at her desk, the reporter retrieved her notes from her purse. They were little more than pieces of paper, sections of sticky notes with her garbled handwriting. Where to begin? This would be strictly follow-up. Her editor had already told her: "No need to wallow in the facts, perhaps a small human interest piece about the camps." She thought maybe there was a bigger story floating around on the bayou. There were certainly plenty of people willing to talk to the reporter about this woman. No one pointing any fingers yet, though, which the reporter found a little strange. They all seemed a little too civil to one another. And when did human nature ever let anyone get the better of it? Chances were good the mother was the one responsible. Yes, that's what human nature would say. The reporter didn't know what to think. She wanted to believe the mother was a better person than that. In a way, it was like all of humanity was riding on it.

Well, dem boys wasn't twins, but most people thought dey was. Jimmy, the oldest, failed first grade. Dey sure is the spitting image of one another. Most people can't tell 'em apart. De only reason I can is 'cause dey spend most of dey time over at my house wid my boys. Dey mama tries hard to provide. Dey ain't got no daddy; most say he run off, but she told me one time, sho, the man was good to her; he just up and dis'peared. Easier say he run off. Be a shame, dem boys done the same thing. She go into town to work. Half the time, Jimmy and Turtle left to deyself. What kind a work she do? You know, waitressing one of dem restaurants off Airline. How long she been doing dat? Oh, hard to say, 'least since I knowed her. Seven, eight years since I move here. Me, following a man, just like her.

The store clerk had looked at the woman like she was crazy, but the woman didn't know what size pants to buy. "Lord," the woman finally said. "They grows so fast."

The store clerk began to rearrange the pants into neat stacks. The woman wanted to ask if the store clerk could wait till she was done.

The clerk's smooth, young hands drifted back and forth into the woman's view. The pants were dropped one by one onto a stack. The slight breeze that this created reminded the woman of church fans; it cooled the woman's concentration. Without asking, the woman took a stack of the khakis and dumped them on the floor. She sat down next to the pants, now at peace. She unfolded one pair at a time, holding them up against the sunlight that fell through the store's window. The shadow of the pants hung on the wall. The woman still searched for the right size.

Baton Rouge, Louisiana—Two young boys went missing Saturday afternoon off Cochon Bayou, in the small town of Lauderville. The boys, Jimmy Smith, 10, and Wilber "Turtle" Smith, 9, were last seen by a neighbor who said the boys were in a small boat, fishing along the shoreline of the lake just before dusk. The mother, Nicolette Smith, came home from work around 11:30 p.m. to find the boat missing from the port. "I had to whistle for a neighbor before I could get home to my camp," she later stated.

When Ms. Smith arrived at home, she was surprised that the boys were not asleep in their bunk beds. After checking with her neighbors, Ms. Smith said she became alarmed and called the sheriff's office.

The sheriff has since said that a boat was sent out immediately to search the area where the boys were last seen, but because it was dark, the search party could make no progress. Early the next morning, the sheriff called in the FBI, who put out an AMBER Alert.

"The mother still believes they can be found," Hawk Hammond, a local sheriff's deputy said. "The boys know their way around these parts."

When asked how long the search would continue, the sheriff's office had no official comment, stating only that "it will continue until it doesn't."

In the next dream, the baby lay face down on a woman's lap. Its feet kicked in the air; its hands scratched and pawed at the woman's's legs. The woman gently patted the baby's behind, as she twisted her lower body from side to side. The baby would not sleep. The remaining women peered down at the baby in amazement, their knives hidden behind their backs.

The mother and the deputies reach a small alleyway along the lower parts of the bayou, where the ripped clothing has been found. There is no other sign of the boys. "These are not their clothes," the mother says. They have come deep into the bayou, where the swamp Maples merge at their tops and cover everything below, where the turtles and frogs and even snakes gladly trot, hop, and slither away. An occasional alligator bumps the crown of its head against the boat's bottom, speaking to the intruders about its kingdom.

"This is the wrong place," the mother says.

The men continue searching with their strong, impertinent eyes.

The mother begins to wish that she and the boys had settled further back, in this place, where people were not as plentiful, where the eyes of the people were not so steadily upon her. She could understand the baser forms of nature here.

"Are you sure," Pup Dan then asks, looking once more at the torn piece of the khaki pant and light blue shirt.

"Yes," the mother says. She turns away then, from the men who persistently watch her and wait for a sign that she has given up.

Hawk and Pup Dan carry each other's glances; they cannot be sure. Hawk spreads the pieces of clothing in his hands, pressing the material flat, allowing the moss-speckled water to drop into the boat.

The reporter makes another visit to the camp. She knocks at the woman's door, but there is no answer. The reporter's gaze lands on the woman's neighbor sitting on her porch on this hot, fly-swatting day. The neighbor says to the reporter, "She gone looking for the boys."

"Where is that?" the reporter asks, as though she, too, will go there.

"About two miles in," the neighbor says. She sits up, whereas she had been leaning back against the old frame of her house. Her chair comes down hard against the floor. The neighbor is dressed in a thin house dress, but it's wide and covers what is beneath.

Looking beyond the neighbor, the reporter sees an endless line of house camps, some sitting briefly above land (until the tide comes in), some with fresh cut yards, others poking out over the water, on stilts that appear too thin to hold them. A small boat motors by and the people onboard wave hello. A white egret stalks along the edges of the water. The reporter can hear cardinals, finches, and woodpeckers calling out. Across the way, she sees moss hanging like a woman's shawl, draped over the crooked limbs of a dead tree. Farther down her sight, she sees an osprey nesting high along the top of a bald cypress. The reporter notices all these things and wonders about the simple, easy life of such people.

Yeah, she done it; who else to blame? No body 'round here got no reason to harm dem childs. Mark my words, yeah, she fess up to it one day; say she just get tied of looking out for dem is all. She be hunting a man soon, yeah. Woman like dat, work her fingers to the bone, fo' what? Most time, dem boys cause ev'rybody plenty headaches. I catch dem stealing rabbits from my pen. When was dat? I say a week or mo'. What I do? Darn near break dey neck, fo' sho. Dey run off to dey mama, cryin'; she don't even whip dem childs, no.

The store clerk had begun to seethe and smolder. The final straw was the woman throwing the store goods on the floor. She wanted to suggest the woman go into town to the Family Dollar store; they, too, carried school uniforms. The woman had never come to the store to purchase her boy's school uniforms before; why today? Especially since the boys still had not been found.

The store clerk walked around the clothes bin, to where the woman sat on the floor, destroying the folds of a dozen or more pairs of khaki pants. "Are you sure I can't help?" she asked, pressing hard on the word "sure."

"I'll find what I need," the woman said.

The reporter's talk with the woman was brief. The woman came back from searching for the possibly dead and was in a crying, angry mood. She cawed at every question the reporter asked. The woman pushed chairs from her path. She picked up, only to sit back down, knick-knacks that could have sat on shelves for years without so much as a dusting. The woman could not sit still. She and the reporter seemed to be playing a game. The reporter wanted to outlast the woman's tempestuous spirit so that she could question her. In the end the woman won: the reporter got up from the sofa when she heard the man who would taxi her back to the dock; he was waiting for her outside. "I better not keep him waiting," the reporter said to the woman and then walked out the door.

When the dream came that night, the woman thought she would wrestle with it, try to push it away. She didn't want to dream about babies and pigs and women with sharpened knives. As soon as her eyes closed, the pig, the women, the rocking baby that would not sleep—all of it defiantly came back to her, a nightmare with no end. The baby's eyes were bloodshot; the eyelids drooped heavily. The baby would sleep soon. The women waited.

Thad's airboat purrs outside the woman's house, the motor a giant fan blowing crinkly ripples upon the water. The bull frog watches from behind the old can, unfazed by the specks of wetness blowing in the air. Inside, the mother prepares for this last relentless effort. She is determined; time has all but run out. But Thad's boat is both fast and capable of reaching the most remote areas of the bayou and swampland in one day.

"Morning," the woman says when she comes out. She leaves the door unlocked behind her.

"Morning," Thad says in return. He looks at his friend, and tries to remember how close they once were. He watches her as she places one foot down in the boat; he hopes he will be the one to find her lost boys.

The woman hops into one of the captain's-style seats. Soon the boat is literally swooning across the water; she swivels but never loses focus of where she is going. The search becomes almost ritualistic: her eyes everywhere, on any small thing that moves or looks extraordinary. They come along a favorite spot on the lake, where she liked to fish while the boys took turns diving off the small boat. The water had always seemed its clearest here, although every area of the bayou seemed to have its own color, all based on the time of day. They had seen navy blue and tea green and ashy gray and fudge black. Two tree trunks marked the spot—they resembled buoys tethering roots below.

"Could you stop for a minute?" the woman says to Thad.

"Sure thing." He pulls the gas lever down, and the boat comes to a gulping halt. It floats up and down over the small but irksome waves it has created.

The woman stands in the open boat. Part of her wants to throw herself into the water. She allows a few tears to leak down the side of one cheek. She wipes the tears away quickly—not that she cares if Thad sees her weakness; she just doesn't want to give in to the mounting sorrow. Some spirit out on the water speaks to her in a clear voice: "If the boys were alive, this is where they'd be."

Thad searches as she does, both of them needling their eyes to go out upon the water amongst the mangroves and the weed-infested shoreline. They search until the sun's glare shoots up from the water and burns their eyes, and blinds them to everything but the dark spots before them.

Getting Stuck at the VA

This creaky, well-used hospital bed is my life raft in a sea of necessary procedures. The bed won't get a bad rap from me. We have become one—welded together by circumstance. The bed is just one (of hundreds) that should have been phased out by my friends at the Veterans Affairs (VA) hospital in New Orleans. I am just one (of thousands) of patients that enlist the services of this aged sickbay. Even the beginning of a new millennium hasn't been cause enough to build a more up-to-date hospital. As we always say, *It will take God's hand to do that.* But, today, I need a major operation. I am fully aware of the VA's reputation; my father was here once and almost didn't make it out. "Cancer of the bowels," they said. It turned out to be a tumor at the back of his neck. Go figure.

So the bed and me, we are best friends since I checked in at 4 p.m. *Don't be late,* my good doctor had said. This I now tell my next door neighbor from across the hallway.

"Late for what," the neighbor asks.

Check in, I say.

"Bullshit," he yells. "Check in when you're good and ready."

Well, I say, *I'm here now.*

My neighbor is very loud. I am certain that all the other patients on this floor hear his every syllable.

"They are coming to take me away soon," he yells.

Oh, good, I say to myself. *I am tired of you already.* But curiosity makes me ask him: *why are they coming to take you away?*

"Because I'm crazy, you fool. Crazy as a fox that's let out all the chickens."

Really, I ask, not quite understanding the fox/chicken comparison.

"Yes, that's right."

But how crazy can he be if he knows he's crazy? I want to ask him this, but I'm afraid. I'm not sure they're coming to get him before night falls, and I would hate to wake up and see his crazy ass standing over me. *Shut up,* I think. *Just shut up.*

They, the NICOM (nurses in charge of me), have stashed me on the fifth floor. *How dubious is that,* I begin to wonder. Immediately, I dial my astrologer/numerologist/psychic/all-around-friend to double-check the significance.

"Get off that floor!" she yells through the phone line. "You know you shouldn't align yourself with any threes, fives, or eights this month."

I press the nurse's button on the side of my bed. After the apparent three to five minutes that's allotted before answering, I hear, "Fifth floor nurses' station, may I help you?"

No, I say, without pressing the button. *Actually, I'm already dead, just forget about it.*

They persist. "Fifth floor nurses' station, may I help you?"

Yes, I say, tentatively. *I was wondering if I could get another room.* Silence from the intercom, but I swear I hear laughing from down the hall. I guess that's a no.

Cheekily, the nurse answers: "We'll check on that, Ms. Sunshine." She lingers on the last syllable of my name, like maybe she's jealous or something. She surely doesn't understand that I am a Gulf War veteran; that I spent two years in a supply tent out in the hot sun of the Arabian desert, before I got hit by a stray bullet; that since then, now that I am home, the VA doctors have found a tumor in my stomach; and that this is the only reason why I am here, in this broken-down hospital. I have no choice, no job, no life outside my family. No, she doesn't understand.

Ten minutes later a nurse comes rolling into my room, forcing her big bulky cart of equipment through the door. (We'll call her Sticker No. 1.) "I've got to get some blood, sweetheart. Okay."

Okay. I'll mention right now that I don't like the blood-giving process. The nurse, the needle, the uncooperative veins, they always conspire to hurt me like no one or thing ever has. This nurse seems capable, but I already know the outcome.

"Arm, please," she says. The rubber thingy is stretched within an inch of its life and then wrapped around my upper arm (my favorite arm, the one I use the most), just above the spot where my timid, shrunken veins are hiding.

That's not going to make them come out, I say.

She continues. "Hold still," as she grasps my arm tighter. She sounds like my mother when I was a child and she combed the kinks out of my hair. If I failed to listen to her, the next step was to yank my head into the position she wanted.

You're the one twisting my arm, lady. Then comes the thumping of the arm. More twisting, before finally, she realizes the dire situation: "You have no veins!" I swear her eyes will pop out of her head. "We need this blood," she says. "We need it now . . . where are your veins?"

I don't know; I left them home? I swear, I said this.

She continues the thumping of my arm with her thin, vanilla wafer colored fingers. Nothing. "Let's check the other arm." Same procedure. Nothing comes. I know she is beginning to think I have no blood.

"Well," she says, exasperated. And so quickly. "I'll be back." Ah, the reinforcements are coming.

Don't hurry, I mutter from beneath the one sheet they've allotted me. I am cold now, with all that poking and sticking. As I lie here, warmed by the slight heat coming from my breath, I think: *Maybe I should pray that she gets attacked by a band of angry patients on her way there.* But I don't. And she doesn't.

TV. *Yes, Lord.* A distraction. The channels are aligned in some type of funky sequence, and there is only one direction (forward), so don't flip too quickly. I miss the answer to a question on *Jeopardy!* right off. By the time I reach the channel again, it is already on commercial. How amazing are the things that you can see on TV? I catch the end of a program about nightingales on PBS. Some are so small they fit into the horns of flowers, sucking delightedly under cover. And wings that rotate so fast that their bodies can hardly keep up. I'd like to fly, fly up out of here.

"Nothing good ever happened at the VA," my neighbor tells me. "Change the channel," he says. "They've got a fistfight on *Oprah.*"

I flip and flip until I've reached *Oprah*, only she's sitting there as calm as a clear day, talking to Dr. Phil—once again—about her own personal problems. *You crazy little man!* I want to yell this across the hall, but don't. Remember, I have to sleep here tonight. I hear him laughing; it's a laugh so strangely poetic that instantly, I am no longer angry with him.

Ten minutes later, I see several nurses gather outside his door. They close the door softly and attempt to speak in a whisper, as if they are preparing for a covert mission. *I can hear you,* I say, but I know they don't hear me. Their voices remain hush-hush:

"Yes, he's got to go."

"Seventh floor?"

"Unh, huh. They called for him already."

"What if he won't go?"

"He'll go."

"He didn't last time. Remember they took him up there by force, and when everyone's back was turned, he slipped back down here."

"You mean he won't stay? Why?"

"Beats the hell out of me, just crazy I guess."

"Well, we gotta do something."

"Can't we wait? The night shift'll be here soon."

"No, seventh floor called for him five times already."

"Okay. So, we just put him in the wheelchair and push him up there?"

Then a voice of reason: "Look, why don't we say we're taking him to X-ray or something? At least he won't cause a scene and when we get him up on seven, Psych can deal with keeping him."

"Okay, sounds good."

In agreement, they open the door and march into the lunatic's room and tell him he needs to go to X-ray.

"All right," he says, "don't you just love going to X-ray?" He waves goodbye to me as they wheel him away. Who said nurses ain't smart? Now, maybe I can watch TV in peace.

A doctor who is not my own comes in, bumps into the slew of nurses carting away my neighbor.

"Hello," the doctor beams.

You are much too happy to be a doctor, I think. He is a Middle Easterner: looks like from way back in the ancient days. He's smiling like maybe he knew Jesus personally.

"How is it you are feeling?" he wants to know.

Fine, but I just got here a couple hours ago.

He looks a bit perplexed, staring back and forth from his clipboard to my strangely calm face. He is salt and pepper bearded and talks in a choppy rhythm.

"I make the rounds," he says.

Really, I think. *What else do you make?*

Laugh now Ms. Sunshine. He doesn't say it but I'm sure he's thinking it. Two days ago I saw a segment on *60 Minutes* or some such show about foreign doctors coming to America, taking up residency slots that American doctors normally get.

So, I ask him straight out, *What brings you to America?*

The perplexed look again. *Job, it is the job,* he manages to say.

So, I say to him: *Did you know that there is a place in India (or somewhere similar) where the Monks are locked up in a small tomb-like shelter with no food and water? They are forced to conserve enough air to last 72 hours. If they are alive when their rescuers return, then they are on their way to becoming high priests or some such thing.* As I tell Dr. Kotabi this, he checks my heart rate. Maybe he already knows about this particular monk ritual. Don't you just hate it when people tell you things you already know? He does, I can tell.

"Breathe in," he instructs. "Breathe out. Sit up. Breathe in. Breathe out. Okay. I am sure doctor, your doctor, comes to see you soon."

Really? I don't believe him. Not because he is a foreigner who talks funny, but because my doctor has already told me he will see me tomorrow, for the surgery.

More TV. More warming of myself under the one measly sheet. And then the biggie happens: I must go to the bathroom. I have already been warned by the NICOM that I am sharing a bathroom with another patient, who happens to be a man. "But he doesn't get out of bed much," they say, sympathetically.

Share? With a man? Is he at least cute, I had asked them. Of course, they didn't answer. I'm not sure why people don't want to talk about such things. But now the moment has arrived. I must get myself to the bathroom without walking in on this possibly gorgeous or ugly man who may or may not be taking care of business when I walk in.

I go bravely, like on *Star Trek*, where no man has gone; but in my case, no woman. I knock, at first softly. Nothing. I knock again to be certain. I enter. ("Lock his door from the inside," the nurses have already instructed me.) I do so now, clicking the large bolt; no one's walking in on me. (They've also told me, "When you leave, be sure to unlock his door so that he will be able to get into the bathroom.") Yes, he will need to gain entrance in his time of need. After I have tinkled briefly (a false alarm), I remember my neighbor, unlock the door, and head back to my life raft of a bed. I move as quickly as possible, lest I pick up some newly formed disease making its way across the browning, tiled floor.

Soon, another nurse comes in. She is different from the one who could not find a vein. Sticker No. 2? She burrows her way in like a middle linebacker for the Saints. Her thick arms precede her no matter which way she goes or how fast. "Let's see what we got," she says, as she grabs my left arm and studies it up and down, twisting me in the process.

Ow! I scream.

She ignores me. "Arm, please." The rubber thingy is stretched again. Literally two thumps from one of her thick fingers against my arm. The needle. Piercing pain. "Oh, God!" (Her.) "Where did it go? I know I had one." Instead of pulling out and giving up, she digs round inside my arm searching for the elusive vein.

Inner and outer screams from me. I am tensing. My left arm is rising. I hope it is readying to beat the nurse repeatedly.

"There," she finally says. The blood trickles into the vial. "What the fu...?" She can't finish, she is so flabbergasted, amazed beyond amazement. The vein closes up shop, refuses to bleed for her. "Come on," she pleads. (Pretty please, with sugar on top?) "No use. This one's a goner." Out she comes with the needle. "Well, I guess we'll have to find another one."

Oh, my God! (Me, this time.) *Somebody help me already.*

She continues her search, in vain. Nothing. "I'll be back," she says. Sure Nurse Roaf. Tell Willie I said hello.

My family calls. They'll be here bright and early—as country folks say, even the chickens won't get up before them. I know that's a lie because those crazy ass country chickens stay awake half the night, cackling and shitting all over the cars parked beneath the oak tree.

Okay, I say. *See you in the morning.*

I love you, my misdiagnosed father adds. I hear my mother in the background… *Me, too.*

Just in case I don't make it through the night? I have to wonder.

I tire of watching reruns and soon fall asleep. I wake up because someone has hold of my arm and is twisting it. *What the fu…?* Sticker No. 3.

"I am the Calvary," he tells me. "If I can't get it, it can't be done."

Well, okay then.

"Arm, please." The rubbery thingy stretches around my upper arm. Thumps. More thumps. "No, no, no. Let's change arms. We may have to go with the hands and then the feet or groin."

What? Good Lord, can't you hear me now?

"Arm, please." Rubber thingy stretches around my other arm. No thumps. But good news. Let's use this one on the side of your wrist.

Okay. I can live with that.

"That's better than having to go to those other parts, yes?"

Yes.

It works. Only one stick and the blood runs freely. I am flowing a river of happy red cells that seem pleased to see the light of day.

"I guess it just needed a little coercion," the Calvary nurse says. "Let's leave this open so we can get an IV set up."

Whatever. You can go away now.

Now that the IV is in and the nurses have stopped waking me, I begin to feel decent about the operation. They will take out the tumor, and all will be well. *This foreign thing will be taken out of me,* I tell myself over and over, and over. Then a late-night visit from an Intern.

"We've lost your original consent form," he says. "We need you to sign another one."

I start to sign, but notice that my doctor is no longer listed as performing the operation.

What the fu …? I insist that my doctor be present and in good working order when my operation takes place.

"Oh, he will be," this youngster informs me.

Where is his name? I ask.

"Here," the Intern says, "here is his name [pointing at the bottom of the paper]. He is listed as the attending."

Just attending, I ask, *or will he actually do what the VA's paying him to do?*

"Oh yes," I'm told. "Your doctor will definitely lay his hands on you, tomorrow."

I don't care for his attitude, but what's a patient to do. Not let it go, that's what. *Will you be assisting my doctor?* I ask.

"Yes, myself and Doctor Logan."

I ask: *As in Brooke Logan* [on the *Bold and the Beautiful*]*? Any relation to the soap actress?* I'm not on drugs yet, so why am I giddy? You are scared, you fool. You are about to hand over your life to a gang of stitching-happy strangers. You can forget your fear if you want to. *Will you promise to take out only what's necessary?* I ask.

"Sure, only what is necessary. Sure thing." Why don't I believe him?

When I finally doze off, around 3:30 a.m., I dream that these doctors' and nurses' strategy is to take out my womb, my womanhood, my link to future generations of Sunshines—my little black box when my life finally goes down. And they succeed. Only later, as my womb lays silent in some aluminum bowl, it suddenly "snaps to" like the real soldier that it is—perhaps recognizing its new surroundings are those of a stranger—and decides to find me. Like a heat-seeking missile it flies out of the bowl, dodging walls and cabinets; and making the sharpest of turns around corners and hallways and lollygagging people, my uterus comes crashing through my locked door. It sits on my bed, a red and snashy figure, shaking like a frightened animal. But I don't know what to do with it. I don't want to tell this frightened ex part of me that I no longer need or want it. When I feel something warm touch me, I think it is my excommunicated womb reaching out to me, but I open my eyes and a nurse stands over me, checking my pressure.

I see my mother's brown shoes standing near the doorway of my room just before they take me away.

"We'll see you when you get back," she says.

Sure, I say. *Sure thing.* And then I'm at the staging area. The operating room must be cleaned, I'm told. A record number of surgeries today. We patients are stacked up like pigs going to slaughter. What a terrible image, I think. Why kill a pig? For the bacon. But, I'm a pig, of the Chinese astrology Pigs. They don't eat those do they? What's really going on?

The anesthesiologist doesn't tell me to count backwards, like you see on TV. "Just breathe naturally and you will fall into a nice sleep," he says. "When you wake up, we'll be all done."

Sure, that's easy for him to say. I breathe but not naturally. I'm falling asleep. *No, wait, wait. I think I've changed my mind…* "Ms. Sunshine, can you hear me? Ms. Sunshine, can you hear me?"

What am I, dazed, finally drugged? Say something to the people!

Yes. Yes. I hear you. I hear you. Oh, my God! The pain!

No one's listening to me. What am I the fly or something? I've shrunken? I'm invisible?

Help. Help. Help. Why do I sound as though I'm whelping?

"We hear you Ms. Sunshine. We are giving you medication now. It will take a few minutes to take effect."

Now? Now? What about before I woke up you idiot interns. I knew my doctor wasn't going to show up for this shit. Now, he would have had sense enough to medicate me before I woke up in all this agony.

"I'm here, Ms. Sunshine." It's my doctor. Oh, okay.

More whelping, trying to elicit sympathy now. *Maybe I can get two doses now?*

"Be patient, Ms. Sunshine. The meds will kick in any moment now."

Help me, you piece of crap doctors. Nurses. Anybody?

"Look," they say. "Here is your family."

Screw my family. I need drugs. My father steps up. He's the one who suggested I come here, reminding me how well things turned out for him. You'll be fine, he had said. He is right not to stand too closely to me. Just out of reach, he struggles to squeeze my arm, throwing his guilty grin all over me.

"How are you feeling?" he asks.

How am I feeling? I need help, can anyone hear me?

"You've got to wait for the medication to work," he says.

Screw you, Father.

My mother steps up. "Just a few more minutes. You can do it."

What, am I giving birth here? *If you don't get me some drugs, I will punch you in the face, mother. I swear, I'll do it.*

She laughs. They all laugh. Traitors.

Within hours I am back on my life raft of a bed, drifting pleasantly away from consciousness. My doctor tells me that the morphine is for pain, but it must be used sparingly. I wouldn't want to become dependent upon it, would I? If it takes away the pain, I will go willingly into dependence. He begins to slip out of the room, but then tells me to press the button whenever I feel the pain recurring. Is he feeling sorry for me? Whatever. You don't have to tell me twice. What he doesn't say is that the morphine dosage is so low that I'll have to press the darn button thirty times to get a decent hit. I'm pressing, and pressing; my finger will become raw. The contestants on *Jeopardy!* have nothing on me. I could go on that show and win hands down. In my current state, I am sure that I know all the answers. I smile to myself for coming to this realization. I know all the answers.

I sleep through most of the next 24 hours. But plenty of nurse stuff happens. A parade of nurses comes through again. I may as well be at Mardi Gras, but without the fun. The Enforcer is first. Slightly taller than average height, a little chunky around the edges, and attitude that she must have inherited from down through the generations. Holy black mother, Batman! She wears an African print nurse's jacket and with her bushy afro, I half expect her to break into a chant.

"You've got to get up out that bed, child."

Already? Shouldn't I be allowed to stay in bed as long as I like.

"No," she answers. "Come on, now, let's get you up."

What, am I shiftless or something?

"No, but you've got to get out of that bed today." She's got to be reading my mind, I'm sure I didn't say that last part.

Leave me alone, you conjure woman! No. She latches onto my arms and pulls. *Oh, my God. The pain. Where is my button? I will press it all day if I have to.*

"No, you won't."

I am standing, and she helps me stay in that position for a few minutes. *Whew!* We both let out the old tired expression. When I was a kid, we used to work the fields. There'd be row upon row of some vegetable or another to pick, and when I made it to the end of a row,

I'd always make that sound: whew! That was back-breaking, *Lord, I've been working on the railroad* kind of tired!

She's taking me way back with all this work, I think.

"Oh, you haven't done nothing, child. Stand up straight!"

Holy bitches from way back, Batman! Couldn't I stay in bed for this? Finally, (minutes later maybe) she tires of torturing me and leaves the room. I try to get back into my comfortable spot. No such luck. I press the button about ten more times.

The Regulator comes in pointing her finger. She's short and fat and sweet smelling, and reminds me of my friend who was kicked out of the army because she couldn't run the PTs.

"You are pressing on that button too much," the Regulator says. "Press once and allow the medicine to work."

Screw you, little fat nurse. I press the button as she clops out the door. Then I laugh a wicked laugh, inside that is. I am winning. I am winning. I press the button all the time. I am winning. All that is left is sleep. More TV. More sleep. I am told that I "cannot eat until maybe tomorrow." Maybe? Whatever. I don't need your stinky bread and your nasty water. Ha, ha. I am winning.

The Good Nurse comes. She is nice. She straps gigantic leg warmers around my legs—it takes her and her helper to get them securely fastened. My legs are now being massaged; in and out the air goes. Oh, you've got my heart, you wonderful nurse. Ooh, how soothing. The Good Nurse likes to talk. I hear her life story. Her Mama's. Her Daddy's. Her cousin's from way back. I don't mind. She is nice. She reminds me of my mother and the way she used to talk when I was a child.

Speaking of mother, I haven't seen her all day. Truth is, now I'm afraid of my family. They came yesterday and almost sent me back to the operating table, this time for my heart. I woke up and they were all sitting in chairs, all of them...the chairs were obviously stolen from other people's sick rooms—generally, they only allow one chair per patient per room. What, is more than one visitor at a time deadly or something? Only the ones who sit down, obviously.

Anyway, they are all big people, but yesterday when they frightened me, they were bigger than usual. I opened my eyes to find them sitting around in these stolen (or borrowed chairs), but slowly, their girth began to grow, as though they were party balloons and air was being blown into them. Pretty soon, they will pop, I thought. I was about to scream when my mother spoke.

"What's wrong?" she asked. "Your eyes are 'most out of their sockets."

No, I said. *It's you. Everyone's blowing up. You're going to pop.*

"Okay," she said. "Go back to sleep."

But they still wouldn't stop staring at me. "What is she doing now?" one asked.

"Look at her eyes; it's like she's looking right through us."

"It's scary, y'all."

"Get the doctor."

"No, leave her be. She just needs some rest."

Screw you family, I heard myself say.

"Screw you," they said.

I've got to learn how to think in a lower tone.

It's 2:30 in the afternoon, eight days after I walked in here, and I'm getting out of this place. My abdomen has healed from the surgery. There is no sign of the tumor. I won't be bearing any children anytime soon, but at least I still have all my parts with me.

It's the Enforcer who finally brings my discharge papers. They're all smiling at me as my sadistic family wheels me past the Nurse's station.

What the fu…? These nurses are glad to see me go?

"The joke's on you," they probably think. "Get out now, Ms. Sunshine, before we send you to the seventh floor."

As we get to the elevator, the Regulator comes running after us. What's she yelling? Apparently, I forgot something.

Oh, no, that's all right, you keep it, I say.

She insists I take it. Oh gee, it's a card that they've all signed wishing me a speedy recovery. Tears swell up at the corner of my eyes. Didn't expect this, but that's the VA for you. What's a patient to do?

Even in New Orleans

Even in New Orleans, I have not found you, though I searched the most likely places. At a welcome home party in the Marigny, someone's copy of the Mona Lisa stared back at me, that little half-smile and supple hands inviting me to stand still for a moment and to try and forget about your beguiling laugh and your own majestic fingers—the ones that once strummed at my ears, which were always hollow with listening for your morning sounds. The people in the background, they tried to tell me that time had already overtaken us, and sent us reeling like fishing lines upon the sea. I would not listen.

I imagined us in Paris making the rounds: daring to plant ourselves at the genuine top of the Eiffel Tower, the evening sun coming down so breathtakingly around us. Losing ourselves in the Louvre, never making it to the East wing to see Rembrandt and all his peers. That moment we stole in a cubby hole near Raphael. The thought replaced your presence in my heart, but only briefly. I then went fully back to craving, wishing, listening, for you.

Sometimes the days of the week seem complacent to me. Get up and move, I'd like to say. Only losers sit around waiting, as though what they've lost will suddenly return. What can I say though? You were a whole life's worth of happiness. Nothing could eclipse you. I will try not to remember that first morning when we met for breakfast. It pains me to think on it. You, in that delectable brown sweater and flip flops. I thought I would fall into the Mississippi with the sudden fit of happiness that shook my old soul loose and set my new itinerary on a path to you. It was a gleeful mood.

Come on, you said, *let's eat.*

Muffulettas for breakfast? I asked.

Sure, why not.

Those long, thin braids of yours had no place falling all the way down your back. Men don't toss their heads like women, my mother used to say. And women don't sit with their legs wide open to the world, you retorted.

My legs will always be open for you, I said.

Always, you asked? And then you tried me.

You keep fingering me and I won't be interested in the real thing, I said.

Oh, yes you will, you said. You pushed your tongue so far down my throat that were you any other man I would have choked, but I didn't because your tongue in my mouth was the most sensuous thing I'd ever known. I could feel you all the way to my clit.

I swear it, I said.

And you said, *yeah, you right*, like you'd been in New Orleans all your life. *I have*, you said. *I was born everywhere and nowhere at all.* I didn't even ask how that could be.

We woke up one morning with the sun burning our backs. We had slept naked on the beach out at the Lakefront.

I miss this, you said.

What, I asked?

Waking up next to you. You asked if I remembered Ponchartrain Park.

How could I forget? I said, as though I had actually lived it and not simply heard about it from my folks. Even though black folks had to use a separate area, they were just happy to have a beach, a cool place to swim.

Yeah, you right, you said again. I saw the memories floating across your temples, as though you had lived it. You said you had. Words, letters and numbers, symbols of happiness. Only your heart was not mysterious.

What a time to go on a memory trip, I said.

No time like now, you said. *Who's to say we got tomorrow?*

Come on, let's get outta here before the pigs come, I said.

You're crazy, you said. *Nobody calls them that.*

I do, I said, and I strutted on off, my big black ass tempting your skinny little hard ass to jump me again, only this time in the beautiful light of day.

I still can't find you, particularly in New Orleans. My friends ask me what happened to you, how come you don't come around no more. They miss your sweet, fine self, but in a different way. They never tasted you and lay pressed upon you so close that your breath wasn't yours anymore.

Where y'at? they say. *Last time we saw that smooth man was a few days before the storm. Where he go?*

How can I tell them that I've lost you? They won't understand how a woman so in love could ever lose track of her man. They'll want to strangle me with their thoughts and doubts about what life really means. You said we were their way out of desperation. Somehow they believed that if you and I found each other, they could find their beloveds, too.

Why not, you used to say. *I'll be their hope and whatever the fuck else they need.*

Today, I walk into the main post office and see some names of the missing tacked up on a board out front. People are demanding that their loved ones be found, even if they have to nail their pictures all over town. How much water can there be in the city after five weeks? The search parties embark each day; some of them never come in. They lay holed up in a boat or on a roof, waiting for daylight so they can pull yet another mother and her children from an attic. They pull bloated bodies from water-filled streets that have merged with the canals. I wonder if they've seen your braids splayed out along the avenues. I place your name on the board, and I wait, though not patiently. I go home, at the Y, where I am staying, sharing a room with three other women like me—homeless, wilting away like dead leaves in the sun.

I try to sleep and you run across my mind like you're wearing track shoes and you're late for a race. I cannot stop you, to talk, to hold you around the waist and plant my kisses upon your chest. You run on, without stopping, without looking back at me. Your face fades like new things in an old house. One of my roommates tells me that this dream means you're gone. If you were still alive, I would see your face, even in my dreams, and you would stop and talk to me. Your arms would embrace me and I would feel safe, like we were holed up in some corner in the Louvre, or on the beach at the Lakefront with sand all up our asses, or on the streetcar making our way up St. Charles just for the hell of it since we knew we'd never ever own a house on that street.

In the meantime, I look across the room and see Mona Lisa staring back at me. That smile. I would like to strangle her. She looks like she knows where you are, but she'll never breathe a word of your whereabouts.

Tonight, I'll dream of you. I'll reach out and pray you'll reach back. Then, I'll sit up on my small bed and I'll conjure you. Soon, your long, hard body will walk towards me. Your braids will be wet; they'll slosh from side to side as you walk. You will not be clothed, for that is the way I remember you lying next to me. *Who needs a bed*, you always said.

Yes, I regret not leaving the city. My family grew up in this town, I told you so many times in those last hours before it was too late to go. I had learned honestly how not to run from hurricanes. But, even my Moms and Pops and sisters and aunties left this time. It was only you and I in the old house. You would not leave me, except to drive my neighbor to the bus station. You didn't come back. Later that morning, the storm sat over the city like it was an angry young woman with nothing else to do. And then the water came, and the streets filled up, with everything: bodies, even houses running away.

If I ask you to come back, I think you should listen. I have things to say to you. I never told you that I would sacrifice everything I have for you. I never said how precious you made me feel even in moments when you stepped away. I never thought to kiss you on the top of your head or just beneath your chin. I didn't make those cookies for your birthday last year. I haven't been back to the Lakefront, I would tell you. There's no use going there without you. I did go to the post office today. I took your picture and placed it with all the others on that board, for everyone who passes by to see that you, too, are loved.

I look at the Mona Lisa and I know all things should be possible. It shouldn't matter if you're somehow lost and can't find your way; you should come back to me. And if I seem complacent in the meantime, or begin to act as though I no longer care, it's only me beginning to give up.

The Old Man's Hands

We both notice the long limbs of Spanish moss hanging from the oak trees along the small state highway. "Humph," the old man says—he is making a mental note of nature's welcome. The old man does things like this: just hauls off and throws out a heavy sigh, or he hiccups way too loud, or, like now, he says things like "humph" to no one in particular but generally he's speaking to me, his son. Sometimes I think the old man does these things because he has gotten too old for his own good. A more likely truth? He needs these moments of quiet attention to keep him company; this is how he reaches out to a world that he thinks is trying to ignore him. This does not stop me from throwing a punishing look in his direction.

We pull into the simple, understated lot of a trailer park. The wheels of my Expedition make a crackling sound as they roll over what must be millions of white gravel shells. I see the ad once more, tacked to the front of a small house trailer to our right. The trailer is all but surrounded—on one side by crepe myrtles losing their last blossoms and on the other by towering shade trees, leaning in and gently touching the trailer's roof and backside. The ad has promised that the trailer would be "in pretty good shape and recently refinished."

A thin white guy comes to the door of the first trailer on our left. He looks about my age—thirty-eight—but he's prematurely gray. He wears loose-fitting worn out jeans and a reddish-white-and-blue plaid flannel shirt, open in the front, with a white T-shirt underneath. He smokes a cigarette as he leans against the door frame; his eyes search my truck like he's intrigued by what he sees. Behind him, through the open door, I see the Confederate flag draped loosely across the back wall of the room.

"Humph," the old man says, and I understand what he means. I wish I had thought to say it first.

The guy drops the burning butt on the step nearest him and smashes it with the tip of his work boot; then he steps fully out of the trailer and walks toward us. His boots munch on the bright white shells on the ground.

"What can I do for you folks?" he asks. He stops a few feet away from my window.

"Looking for a trailer for sale; saw your sign up at Wal-Mart in the city," I say.

"Over this way," the guy says, pointing his finger to the miniscule trailer I noticed when we first pulled in.

I get out and walk to the passenger side of the truck. The old man has not stepped one foot outside. He hasn't even opened the door. He sits, leaning his head back against the seat, his lips moving, and although I cannot hear him, I know he's already making up reasons why he won't like "this one." This is the third trailer (possible lodgings for him) that we've looked at; this time, we've come forty miles outside New Orleans.

"Get out, old man," I say, and stand there waiting for him to move.

I can't remember the last time I called him "Dad" or "Pop," or some such affectionate term. All I know is that when I was a kid, the old man would taunt me, in so many ways. The most hurtful was when he refused to call me by my name, Ron. Instead of Ron, he might say, "Hey, boy," or "Little boy, go do this or go do that." It must have given me a complex—it got to where I'd rather he call me nothing at all than have him screw with me like that. When I got older, I started calling him "old man," in retribution at first, but later just because I could. The old man accepted the reversal of situation easily enough, as if to say he could care less one way or the other. The funny thing is that over the years, he somehow lost track of his true name, like it was bandaged up in the scabs of his memories, and now if someone asks his God-given name, more often than not he has to search his recesses to come up with a name he has had for eighty years. And when he looks to me for help (his eyes asking me to speak for him), I find that I have selectively forgotten as well.

Sometimes I imagine he likes being called "old man." Like when visitors come to the house and one of the first things they see is the Xeroxed copy of the old man's hands on the wall. Inside the frame is a picture of the old man, solemn and facing the world like he knows it particularly. Oddly enough, he is still handsome, his facial features are just beginning to drift downward. He is barely gray, and then mostly around the edges in sections, like the leftovers of snow on the ground. In the copy the old man's hands are open with the thumbs placed closest to his face, almost touching his ears. Usually, when visitors see this framed photo of him and his hands, they might think of the beginning months of life when a father or mother or some other such relative or friend of the family might stick their thumbs in their ears and wiggle and wave their fingers until a jolly little baby laughs and laughs and laughs, uncontrollable. These visitors are instantly taken back to those early days of their own lives, and the joy of remembering such moments always makes the visitor smile. At such times, if I am quick enough, I look over at the old man and catch him smiling, too. I am always amazed that he finds a way to place himself nearby, on the sofa, or as he says, "just happened to come from the kitchen," for moments such as these. He's a junkie for that inevitable smile.

Both the old man and I stand with our hands clasped at the back of our waists, our elbows jutting out like skeletal wings. Neither of us speaks as we wait to be let into the trailer. The guy, who we've surmised is the proprietor of the lot, has gone around to the back window to let himself in. Apparently, his teenaged daughter has let someone see the trailer just yesterday, and she forgot to replace the key beneath the Easter-colored watering tin at the base of the steps of the only door of the trailer.

We hear footsteps inside and then the door swings open. Without speaking, the guy turns and leaves us to enter or go as we please. I hold the door for the old man, and he nurses himself up the brief steps, favoring his left leg, which was nearly shot off in World War II, and which, even though the leg has healed, still causes the old man pain.

Although the temperature is quite cool outside, when we enter the trailer, a suffocating warmness greets us. There is a smell associated with the heat, as though one birthed the other. At once, I understand the ad's suggestion that the trailer had been "recently refinished." Sheets of shiny new paneling have been spread over the entire living area, just barely bypassing the light-green kitchenette, but then leading into the small bedroom at the back of the modest trailer. The ceiling has been repainted white, but the one coat is not enough to cover the years of wear and use underneath. The ceiling also droops in the middle. Other than these things, the floor feels solid beneath my feet. I imagine that it has been replaced at least once.

"How old is the trailer?" I ask the guy, who stops walking toward the bedroom and turns to me.

"Don't rightly know. It's been here since I can remember."

"Humph," the old man says.

I say nothing. We resume our short trek to the bedroom. On the left, just beyond the kitchenette, is a small bathroom, with a toilet, a sink, and the thinnest shower I have ever seen. Instinctively, I look at the old man. I realize at once that he could just barely fit into the shower, but in my mind, I am already envisioning him in this trailer, out of my house, living his own life.

"That tile is fairly new," the man says as he passes the bathroom.

I look closer at the mauve colored tile that covers the bottom half of the walls. My reasons begin to pile up, so that I can use them in defense when the old man complains about the trailer. "But what about that beautiful tile in the bathroom?" I will say.

The bedroom has recently-vacuumed, shaggy brown carpet on the floor, and I am sure my father is about to grunt, or stomp, or do something disruptive because he hates what he calls "fat carpet." The richer and deeper it looks, the more he can't stand it. I think it goes back to his childhood, when his family barely "had a pot to piss in," as he says. "We learned how to live simple, not like we was better than nobody else." And time after time, I would say, "But the world has changed, old man." Over the years, he's held on to those old ways like they were precious.

"All the paneling is new," the guy says, and I want to tell him how unnecessary his words are. The paneling stands out, like it's hiding the true nature of the trailer. One is left to wonder, "What's behind that paneling?" The guy situates himself in the corner near the window that he must have used to break into the trailer. I get the impression that he's not comfortable, like he's standing near the window in case he has to use it again, but this time as a quick escape. For a moment, I question why I feel this way. Am I holding on to the old prejudicial ways of thinking, of protecting myself? Of protecting the old man? I know that the old man never quite got over growing up in the South. Of all his stories, the ones he seems to remember the most are of the many days when, as a young black boy, he worked plowing the fields of some white farmer or another, and earning just two bits, or four bits if he was lucky.

I am literally standing there in this white guy's trailer thinking of these things when I sense that the old man has walked over to the window and begun to inspect it with his eyes, then his hands. He runs his fingers down the outside borders of the windows, no doubt feeling for cracks where the wind might come in. When he is finished with one side, he goes to the other side —almost pushing the guy out of the way. He has gotten a little impatient in his old age.

"Where you folks coming from?" the guy says, perhaps out of a newfound interest, or just to make conversation.

"The Eastbank," I say, with emphasis, so that my words carry all the weight of Hurricane Katrina and what it means to still be living in East New Orleans five years later.

"You don't say," is what the guy says. Then, he adds, "You'll have to move the trailer." He looks at me, without turning away. I wonder if he's looking for a tell-tale sign that I've been offended, or not.

I haven't been. "I guess the $2500's negotiable?" Now, it's me looking at him, waiting for an answer.

The old man continues his inspection of the bedroom. His hands slide across the paneled walls. He creeps like the woman in that story I read in college, although there is no yellow wallpaper on the wall. I wonder if the old man is searching for the soul of this place; I know he needs to feel that he belongs. Maybe he's just looking for some new thing to grab hold of, and if he finds that thing, he may finally feel at peace.

The old man placed the Xeroxed copy of his hands in the picture frame a few months after he and I had finally made it back home after Katrina. He had been living with my wife and I for a few years—since he lost his wife (my mother) in the flood. I believed he was over the loss, and "all that business" with Katrina, as he often called it. He would have these bad days when he relived the grief. He started to behave in unbecoming ways. Like the useless remarks and loud noises he would raise, and at the most inconvenient times. He often sat in front of the TV and watched televangelists all day long. All of them promised him a pain-free life, if only he would send them money. One told him to make a copy of his hands and send it, with a small donation, to a disclosed address. The old man believed that all his problems—anything, from lack of money to pain and suffering—would disappear.

That night, when I came home from work, the old man insisted that I take him to the nearest Kinko's to have his hands copied. While there, he made about twenty copies, in case the first ones were lost or this whole procedure didn't work the first time. The idea had already sprouted that he would send a copy to other televangelists as well, whether they requested it or not. After the old man sent in the first copy of his hands, a few weeks passed without any word or any change in his situation. He still moped around the house, apparently feeling as lost and depressed as he had before. He sent in a second copy—this time, with a $6 donation—but he got the same results. On the third try, he sent $7, and on the fourth, $8, increasing his donation by a dollar each time.

One night, after about six months had passed, and the old man's donations had increased to $10 and his situation hadn't changed in the slightest, I walked through the door (after a day of hard work) and there on the wall was the picture of the old man. On either side of the old man's face was a copy of one of his open hands. The thumbs sat so close to his ears that I immediately thought of parents and that thing they do when they try to make their baby laugh by sticking their fingers in their ears and waving them back and forth. I couldn't help but smile. And wouldn't you know it, the old man was standing there smiling back at me.

According to the old man, it was the healing promises that had brought a smile to my face. I had no such proof or belief. Since I lost my mother in the flood waters, I have doubted the existence of many things—the healing of human beings in pain is one of those things.

I wonder about the forgiveness we give or deny God. The only thing I knew, that first time I walked through the door and found the old man smiling back, was that sometimes life grants us a ray of sunshine on an otherwise dismal day. I didn't know why, but I wanted the old man gone then. I have since realized that I still hadn't forgiven him for being the one to live, instead of my mother. Why did he hold on when life was choosing whether or not to let go of him?

I feel the leafy limbs of the shade trees glide along the flattened top of the trailer; they are being swept back and forth by the wind's power. The old man's eyes peer up, as do my own, as do the other guy's, as if to acknowledge that God has spoken. I imagine it was these very trees that protected the trailer from Katrina's full force.

"Won't be easy to move it from this spot," I say. I suddenly feel odd about removing a thing that has been planted so long.

"One way or another," the guy says, "these old trees'll be cut down, if we need to."

"Humph," the old man says, and I know he is feeling the same empty, sour feeling at the pit of his gut that I feel. We both share a love of nature, and the thought of these aged trees being sacrificed for some small sense of comfort for the old man and I, well, it begins to weigh on us, heavily. We begin to ask ourselves, what might we gain from his living in this trailer and me living in the house?

"There's no way to leave it here?" I ask, considering the full possibility that the old man could move here, and finally and thoroughly be on his own. I feel his eyes on me. I hear his thoughts trying to find me and spank me like he did when I was still his little boy. And for some reason, I remember a day when I was very young and the old man was talking to a man he met on the street. I stood leaning against the old man's leg, and at some point, he reached down and placed his large hands on my head. His fingers cupped my head like it was a small melon. "This is my boy," the old man said. Here now, I can feel the pride that went into the old man speaking those words. I think back to all those times he called me boy instead of Ron. Could it have been his way—his "term of endearment" for me? I am not so sure. This memory from long ago sends pangs of guilt beating against the remaining core of my heart.

"Sorry, can't do it," the guy says, bringing me back to reality, back to the present. His eyes do definite battle with me now. I am trying to figure out if he means it sincerely, or if it's a made-up lie. I imagine that he's trying to figure out whether or not this is the deal-breaker. From the corner of my eye, I see the old man has stopped caressing the walls and now stands facing me. His arms are crossed, which means things could get ugly real quick. The only opinion that means anything is the old man's—whether or not he could live in this place, I mean.

"Well, I suppose someone will buy the trailer sooner or later, and the trees will be cut down no matter what," I say, speaking to the old man.

"Humph," he says.

We walk back through the trailer, pass the tiny bathroom with mauve tiles, then the light-green kitchenette; then in unison, we all stop, our eyes finding the bright new paneled walls of the living room. I search the ceiling once more, perhaps reminding myself that what lies beneath this newly finished interior cannot be covered up forever. I imagine the middle of the trailer eventually falling in, perhaps sooner than later. I imagine the old man sitting on the new sofa we will need to buy, watching his old TV. I see him eventually getting used to the sad smell of the place. I see him caulking the windows in the bedroom. I see him get used to not being able to throw up his hands if he wants to as he's taking a shower. I can see him living in this imperfect place, trying to make a more perfect life on his own.

One thing I can't see is the old man's smile when I come home from work and walk in the door, and see that same Xeroxed copy of the old man's hands, the thumbs almost sticking into his ears, reminding me that I was once so young that this man took care of me. I imagine how sometimes he would stick his thumbs in his ears and wiggle his fingers so that, as a baby, I could not control myself. I would laugh a child's laugh. I wonder if I'll get used to not seeing the old man's smile.

"What do you think?" the guy asks, impatiently. I understand that he is waiting for our decision. I understand how difficult it must be to let strangers walk over his belongings. This waiting act humanizes the man, so that I no longer question his motives. It's all about selling this trailer, to whoever will buy it. Why do we get caught up in people's motives, I wonder.

I look over at the old man, who is also waiting for my answer. His stoic posture says he knows I am the one who wants this, not him. This small truth is finally evident to me as well.

"Let's go, Pop," I say, as I find myself walking down the brief steps that lead off beyond crepe myrtles that are showing their last color. I don't have to look back because I know my father is walking briskly behind me. I can feel him there, hear his feet shuffle to a new beat. Or perhaps it is an old tune that both of us had forgotten.

David and Michal

David: What if you were questioned on every fucking thing you do?

Michal: We all are, David. *(She is trying to talk him down, to calm him, but it isn't working.)*

David: All I know is it's 20 fucking oh-8 and you'd think people had better things to do than fuck with me. I see more than they know.

Michal: The hill thing, right? Yes, I know. I know, David.

David: *(Ignoring her)* I see them coming up the hill after me. I'm climbing, I'm climbing. It's a big-assed hill, and I can't get to the top with Solly pulling me down. *(Solly is his word for "the man"—every organization, department, or individual set on thwarting his progress is Solly. It has been this way since he was a teenager about to go out into the world to make his way as a man.)*

Michal: What do you want me to do, David? *(She thinks that if she keeps him calm, everything will be okay.)*

David: I want you get the fuck off me.

Day.

They walk the two blocks down Rocheblave to Canal St. and board the first streetcar that is heading in the direction of the river. The streetcar is crowded enough that they have to remain standing in the aisle near the front. The windows are down because it's springtime and the humid summer weather has not yet arrived, and because the tourists like to sit with their heads and arms and half of their bodies hanging out the windows in hopes of getting a more perfect view of the new and improved New Orleans they've come to see. But even with the cross breeze making its way in and around the crowd of passengers, there is an old smell that lingers, something like half-cleaned urine mixed with last week's cabbage. David and Michal share looks of displeasure. Almost immediately, their eyes go in concert to the older white woman sitting directly across from them on one of the handicapped seats. They know her; they have actually named her Mrs. Greedy because she never gets enough of riding the streetcar. Every weekday morning around ten o'clock, she gets on at the turnaround near City Park and rides the route up and down Canal St. until late afternoon, when, David and Michal have often surmised, she goes back home, prepares and then eats herself a nice bowl of cabbage and rice, and then readies herself for the next day's ride. They do not lock eyes with her, though, for she is liable to take their stalled glances as an invitation to talk, an opportunity for her to tell them how her husband died in the same year that Big Bush went to war in Iraq, and how she's been alone since then, except for the Sisters at St. Mary's who come and visit her once a week, on Saturdays, and how she'll be seventy-one years old in December and she still has her own teeth, and how she likes to ride the streetcar because she can meet people from all over the world, and how they can meet her, too, and go back to their hometowns and tell others about meeting her. Someone will inevitably catch her attention, and everyone within listening distance will hear the same stories again. And David asks, when they get off at Decatur, "If she wants to meet people from all over the world, how come she don't get the fuck off the streetcar?" and then Michal laughs at the older woman's sad folly and because she wants to please David. Michal and David, both in their late twenties, think, "This will never be us." They get off the streetcar and walk into the French Quarter, all cocky, like they've won a million dollars each. They walk. But Michal's mind doesn't rest.

She thinks about her music class and all the notes on the piano she has not yet learned. She wishes David could help her more. He is the one who was a year away from getting his Music degree from Dillard; he is the one who has led her here—over ten months ago, on an absolutely lazy morning in bed when neither of them had a job. He blamed the steady flow of immigrants into the city since Katrina for his fate, and tried to convince her, especially when he wanted to lay with her, that he wants to work but that there is no work for which he is ultimately qualified. He hasn't even been able to look at a piano since Katrina. But he takes her on, "as his project," and reminds her about the city and other kind souls building houses for musicians. "They'll always take care of the music," he said.

"But you know I can't play," she had reminded him.

"You can train. I can help you," he had finally said, and then lifted himself off the mattress that lay on the floor and walked into the bathroom.

They had only known each other for a year then, and she was still fascinated with how perfectly formed his ass was—so hard, and raised high like a house on stilts. She would often linger behind him when they walked together—to the corner Quik Stop for cigarettes, down to Van's for snowballs topped with condensed milk, or farther down the street to his friend Johnnie's apartment, just to sit around the front stoop and talk shit—and as she remained one step behind him, all that she wanted to see was his ass beating strong like a heart in winter, about to stretch out of his jeans, and leaving her pleased and satisfied to be a woman. Back then, when they would make love, she would place her warm hands at the base of his bare naked cheeks, at the spot where his butt curved into the back of his upper thighs. After he had entered her, as he pushed and gnawed deeper and deeper into her soft insides, she would allow her mind to peacefully break away. And what she thought about was how perfectly they fit together. In her mind, she saw them always together.

She can't help but notice that David spends most of their walk looking about him for any suspicious movements from the strangers that he meets. "Where you going, man?" she overhears someone say. There are three black teenagers, all dressed in white t-shirts and blue jeans, ready to elude the police if they need to. They continue down the street; none of them turn back to look at she and David. "Fucking Solly," David says, but Michal thinks that the way he says it sounds more like he bears these boys in his heart, closely, remembering that he was one of them not so long ago—walking the streets when they should be in school, sometimes with a Glock stuck in the back of their waistbands, looking for any sign of trouble. Michal shudders, trying to shake off the possibility that this man, her man, would secretly wish he could join the boys and for just one more time feel what it was like to be so young and able to say, "Fuck whatever happens next." She thinks of David's headaches, which have gotten worse, and the times she has woken up in the middle of the night to find him leaning over her, staring into her half-opened eyes. She knows something is turning him inside out, but she can't get him to see this. And when she asks him to go to the hospital, he shrugs her off.

Michal throws away these thoughts like they are trashy and unclean, placing her mind back on this street, on her walk with David. She knows he is simply happy that she is finally taking the music classes and that he can walk with her to her private lesson every day. Her eyes go over to David, there on the street, walking past Canal Place. When they are together like this, she feels that all the world is for them, wants them to make it.

Looking about her, she can smell the Mississippi River, it's so close. She hears the sound of the ferry docking behind them. Soon the cars and passengers will come rushing out like a great whale regurgitating untasty morsels onto the shore. She is wearing the short, black skirt that David likes. It accents her legs, he always tells her. He believes her legs belie her age. They are long and cut firm like an expensive cut of meat. "You look like you used to running from something, baby." And even though she doesn't like hearing this from him, she does appreciate the fact that he notices her; that when they're walking down the street as they are now, she knows he can't help but notice her.

Part of her understands his need to know what happened in her past. "You must have done a lot of skipping town to get to wherever you was going, right baby?" This is what people always said about women who had to rely on a lot of men to get by. "It's something about the way your lips curl when you look at me," he once told her. "It's like you studying up trouble with me in it." She had long ago told him about her mother, who had been brought up in one of those deep country towns in Louisiana where they knew how to throw a hainch, or spell, on a man or woman or child, and wouldn't think twice about it. Michal still wouldn't eat anybody's red gravy but her own. "You never know what another woman might throw in there," she had once told David. "And if a woman put a little bit of her own fluids in her sauce, you're sure 'nough in for some trouble." He had laughed at her then, and asked what kind of fluids? When she whispered in his ear what she meant, he fell off the chair laughing. She knew he did so out of discomfort as much as his sudden need to chuckle about this raw truth that now ran between them. Michal could easily be one of those kind of women.

Michal's mother had taught her how to please a man. And this was the thing about her that David did appreciate. Michal's mother had told her: "If you know how to tighten your pussy, you can keep a man happy no matter how old you get." Her mother had been in her late sixties when she told Michal this, and still had a strong line of satisfied men getting up from her bed. David often said to her, "The thought of sex with you at sixty, baby, is definitely a turn-on; that's no lie."

As they walk together, Michal's thoughts slip to a silent awe of this pretty and clean new city that has risen as if from the ashes since Katrina. She notices that some things never change. Jackson Square is still as crowded with tourists as it ever was. Couples still sit close at Café du Monde, with sprinkles of powdered sugar on their glad cheeks and their sightseer clothes. They stand in lines at the daiquiri bars and dart in and out of the souvenir shops. And down every perpendicular street that she and David pass, she notices that Bourbon St. is full to bursting with revelers. The people come down the side streets in little streams, escaping from the sinful acts that may have kept them on this old and weathered street, much like water that leaks from a levee.

Michal and David walk through the French Market until they reach Esplanade. They always take the scenic route to get to Mrs. Clouatre's. Within a few blocks, they stand at the bottom of the steps that lead up to the renovated, raised house. It looks a bit stifled and unnatural from the bottom looking up, painted in shades of green, yellow, and purple, as though Mardi Gras season never left. David isn't watching the house though. He has often told her that he likes the way her legs march defiantly up the elongated set of steps. "The back of your skirt bounces up and down, and leaves this small opening and closing window. And then something moves around in me. You know what it is, baby?"

And she asks him, "What?"

"It's your pure, sweet ass turning me on, that's what." Every time he tells her this, she laughs. "And then you know what I do then?" he always says.

"What?" She is happy to encourage him with this foolishness.

"I don't get ashamed of it, that's for sure. I just reach my hand inside my pocket and push it over to a more comfortable spot, where it stay until you get your ass home again."

Whenever they have this conversation at home, it always leads to sex—sex as rich and tasty as a bouillabaisse sauce.

As Michal's steps cross the porch, Mrs. Clouatre opens the door. She has somehow heard Michal even before she gets there. Michal smiles, for she is glad to have this aging and magnificent woman as her private piano teacher. Ms. Clouatre sees David standing at the bottom of the steps and she summarily waves a wrinkled, Creole hand to him before she pulls Michal into the house.

"Come in quickly, cherie," she says. "We can't let all the good fortune escape, can we?"

"No, Ma'am," Michal says, and disappears behind the closing door.

Evening.

Michal is trying to clear her way from the older woman's house. She knows that David will be worried about her and will catch the streetcar to fetch her home soon.

"I really must go," she tells Mrs. Clouatre.

"I know, cherie, but I worry about you with that man."

"Why?"

"Why? Why, this here girl wants to know. You don't have to tell me, but I sense something is wrong there."

Michal wants to run and hide from this truth. She says nothing more to Mrs. Clouatre. She walks out of her teacher's house and begins her journey back home to David.

After Michal has gotten off the streetcar, she walks briskly down the street until she hears the unmistakable voices of David and his friend Johnnie. She knows they are sitting out on the steps in front of the shotgun house she and David call home. Instead of marching on steadily until she reaches them, Michal slows down and listens intently to the conversation between the men.

"Where's your woman, man?" Michal knows Johnnie is always trying to get a fix off David's troubles.

"Don't know, Johnnie," David then says. "Seems like ever since she started those music lessons, she never home before dark."

"Sounds like another nigga, man."

"Fuck that. She'd better get her old ass home if she need a whipping."

"Ah, man. You talk like you know something."

"I know Solly better keep his hands off my woman."

"Fuck Solly."

"Fuck you," Michal hears David characteristically respond. She has seen David and his friend sit on these steps many times before, seemingly oblivious to the world around them. They sit talking, insulting each other, berating "the establishment," and all in the name of waiting for her to come home. This ritual has become like a game that these two lifelong friends play. This particular conversation is the same one they've had for the past few weeks. Michal thinks the two men know each other so well their relationship is like going to church. They've grown up worshipping each other's presence. They tell each other the same jokes and the same sad tales; yet, it always sounds new to them.

Johnnie's old man was actually the original Solly. When they were teenagers, and David had just moved to New Orleans, Johnnie's father would turn out the lights in the early evenings, so that if David stopped by, he wouldn't know anyone was home. David caught on quickly enough. Sometimes he would stick around outside their house, waiting for Johnnie's father to stop bullshitting and let him in. She listens to the two men talk about it now, as though neither has heard the story before, or as if they've heard it so many times before that they can't help but tell it over and over again, like it is water for their thirsty survival.

"Yeah," Johnnie says, "my old man used to hate you."

"You don't have to tell me. That was fucked up."

"He thought you would bring me to 'ruin and damnation' is what he said."

"It was the other way around, nigga."

"Yeah, I admit it. Hey, you remember the time you stood outside singing until my old man got so pissed, he come storming out the door like he was gonna bust you in the ass?"

Johnnie begins to laugh tentatively, waiting to see if David will do the same.

"How can I forget it? That was the first time I ever sang a church song that long." David's laugh joins in with Johnnie's, and they sound as though they have formed their own choir of laughter.

"What was that song, man?"

"Pass me not, 'O Gentle Savior'."

"Yeah, I remember now. Every time you got to 'Hear my humble cry,' you'd hold the note so long, like you was really crying, man. Shit, that was funny. I was sitting on the sofa next to my old man, and he grabbed me by the back of my neck 'cause I was laughing so hard."

Johnnie's laugh is like a howling wind now; it comes in spurts and gets louder the longer he laughs. His eyes close and open and set over his round, light brown face, which has begun to attract freckles around his cheeks. He could be a black Howdy Doody.

David can barely speak, he's laughing so hard. "I know. I know. I could hear him telling you, 'Shut up, boy! Now he know we in here.'"

"Yeah," Johnnie finally says. "Them was some crazy times."

"Yeah, nigga, that shit was real funny."

As their laughter and memories die away, back into the recesses of all they hold dear, Michal notices that the evening has darkened so much that all the graceful shades of sunset have disappeared behind the beaten up houses and oak trees that line the street. Michal knows that she must go to David then; she feels it in her bones, way down thick, that he is waiting for her.

When she appears beneath the street light just down the street from where the men sit, she knows she must act as if she is transplanting nature's beauty with her own. When David sees her, she does not want his eyes to leave her as she draws closer. She walks purposefully, like she is a cat that is coming home after a day spent playing with lithe, sexual cats like herself. She must wear her sensuality and never allow it to be lost in the likeness of all those other women. One of her legs must gently lead the other; one hip must slowly dance with the other. She feels their eyes on her now.

When she reaches David and Johnnie sitting on the steps, Michal says, "I can hear y'all laughing all the way down to the Quarter."

Though both of them might think it, David is the first to say, "Fuck that."

She waits for one of the men to get up and allow her to pass, but she knows that David will not be able to resist putting his hands on her, that he will not allow her to go into the house and do her womanly things. Neither of the men moves. Their defiant eyes remain on her. Their bodies sit erect, like shields ready to repel her. It is as though they have read each other's minds and know what is expected of the other: to keep her from moving past them.

"May I get by," she says, playing their game.

"Fuck no," Johnnie answers.

David says, "Shut up, nigga," without looking at Johnnie. She knows that David has playfully embarrassed Johnnie into silence. She leans into David then, as though she will push her way through the wall the men have set up.

David asks, "Where you been? I was worried."

"I been at Mrs. Clouatre's all afternoon; you know that."

"I don't know shit, baby." And then he smiles and shows his wide mouth full of white, white teeth that glare up at Michal.

And she falls into him, with one of her arms around his shoulder; in the other hand she holds a bottle of Beaujolais. And he kisses her just beneath her chin, and further down her neck, until she tells him to stop. But he won't, because he has been waiting for this moment since he saw her come out of the dark ambience of the evening, walking to him, leading on the very urges that she had given him earlier in the day.

She wants him to hold her there for as long as he likes—until he has taken in the whole sweet and musky scent of her, and tasted the full nature of her body melting on his tongue. "Hold it, yes, just there," she says, as if he lives on just her air. She wants him to get so caught up in the moment that he won't see the two middle-aged men that are walking by; for if he sees them, he will fall into one of his fits again.

But David does see them and quickly pushes Michal away from him. He stands up as though he will confront the men. But they have both gone on and are walking absentmindedly down the street.

Michal pulls gently on his shoulder.

"Solly," he says. "Asking me where the money was." He then sits back on the step, reluctantly, and his eyes follow the men until they disappear in the early darkness.

Michal and Johnnie send a suspicious glance each other's way. Michal wants Johnnie to be gone, to leave and go home just this once, so that she and David can sit and talk.

But Johnnie sends support to his friend: "Yeah, them bitches is gonna come one day, man and we gonna punk their asses."

"Shut up!" Michal lashes out. "Don't you have somewhere else to go, Johnnie?"

Then David is between them, like he must always remain between them. He stands with his back to his friend and he faces his woman. Michal isn't surprised when David tells her, "Leave this fucking nigger alone. He'll go home when he feel like it."

He has hurt her, though she decides to stand there solidly, to take her place in this man's world, like her mother always told her to do. She can even hear her mother's echoing voice, "Girl, don't take no shit from no man. You hear me?" But her mother's voice is so far away.

She pushes her way through the men, walks up the three steps, and opens the screened door of the house. "If only he'd come inside and help me with my music," she thinks. But she knows how much he detests any part of him that ever wanted to play music, ever wanted to be someone other than a street kid with no options. She wishes she could take this chip off his shoulder; this belief he has that no one ever gave him a chance, even after he'd begun college—no one would take him seriously, not the way he wanted. He was a grown man and didn't think he should still have to play pick-up on the streets in the Quarter for money, dancing around and strumming on the guitar and keyboards for the tourists like he was a monkey for hire. He always blamed her for not being able to see that. "I don't have those dreams anymore," he would tell her. "It hurts to think that I ever did."

Michal turns to David before she enters the house: "You coming in?"

"When I'm ready, aiight?"

Although David is watching her, Michal knows he can't see how her spirit just slips and falls to the floor. She feels like a stone that has been dropped into a pool of water, going deeper and deeper toward the bottom—she has no expression to match what she feels inside, just a lifeless stare which sits much too comfortably on her face. She has nothing left to do but walk into the house. David has taken away some of her options, not only for this moment, when he has disrespected her and personally reduced her to a lesser being, but for tomorrow and the next time she dares believe there is perfection to be had with him. The worst part of it is that he doesn't understand just how much he is breaking her.

As she disappears into the darkness of the unlit room, she knows that David will eventually tell Johnnie to leave.

David will first offer his tightly closed fist to Johnnie, and they will dap and signal each other that it is time to part.

And Johnnie will say, "Lord, watch between us," as he walks away.

"You got it," David will say. "Till we meet again." And David will come in to her and try to make right what he has tried to destroy earlier.

Night.

She can hear the television in the other room. David is watching a special report on WDSU about the New Moon Festival that's been going on in Woldenberg Park. People from all over the world, but especially California—the old beatniks and moon watchers of the sixties—are in town for the festival. They have eaten the best that the famed restaurants in the city have to offer. They have drunk strawberry wine left over from the Strawberry Festival. They have stood in crowds like waves of willful listeners, intent on hearing Irma Thomas and bands like Rockin' Doopsie. They have smoked their joints in the clear of day, passing their temporary high over to their neighbors. And they have danced in twos and threes and even fours and fives, swaying to no particular beat, their eyes plastered on the gigantic moon resting above their heads.

Michal looks out the window, and indeed there is a full moon sitting brightly over the city. The thought of it makes her melancholy, and she suddenly wants to cry tears that will never end. She is still raving over David's treatment of her, and in front of Johnnie, no less. "I can do better than this," she finally says, to the air, to no one in particular.

David turns off the TV in the other room. When he comes into the bedroom, she turns away from him.

He lays himself down on top of the bedspread, next to her. Speaking to her back, he says, "You ever notice that there's news on TV morning, noon, and night. And evening?"

Michal ignores him.

David continues: "I mean, how come they need so much news? I guess there's always something happening. Solly is busy; that's what I say."

He lies there for a moment before he asks, "What y'all do over at Mrs. Clouatre's?"

It takes a moment, as if she is deciding whether or not to answer him, but she finally says, "Practicing. That's what I go over there for."

"Yeah, but you can't be practicing half the day, Michal."

After another sound silence: "We talk, too."

"About what?"

"Just women things."

"Like what?"

"I don't know David," and with this she turns to him and her face is only inches from his. "We talk about a lot of things."

He is persistent: "Like what?"

"She thinks you're going to hurt me one day."

"And why would she think that?"

"She is an old woman who sees things."

"Well, she can't see too much, Michal. She ever think you'll be the one to hurt me?"

"David, why on earth would you say that?"

"When it comes down to it, baby, you're no different than the rest of them."

"Solly, you mean?"

"Who else?"

Michal closes her eyes then, and David gets up from the bed and walks into the bathroom.

When Michal opens her eyes again, David is standing in front of her. He is as naked as when he came into the world. He stands waiting, as if he wants her to see him, all of him, and to want all of him, no matter how sorry and pitiful he was to her earlier. He doesn't say, "I'm sorry, baby. I just wasn't myself tonight. This thing in my head has me doing things even I don't know how to explain." He simply slides himself beneath the covers with her, pushing her over slightly, so that his body rests on the edge of the mattress. He reaches for her, like he always does, with a touch that says he is praying she will reach back.

"I'm not in the mood, David."

He pretends he doesn't hear her and begins to pull at the oversized t-shirt she has worn to bed. She pushes his hand away. He moves his hand up and down her back.

"Come on, baby. What's this? You're gonna let me in, ain't you?

"No, David. I'm not kidding. Leave me alone."

But there is no way for him to go away from her and leave her alone. He is solid, hard by then. She can feel him pulsing against her leg. She feels weak then. She will invite nature inside, and it will not disappoint her. Michal begins to give up her willpower. David will eventually have her.

She believes she loves him. Besides, she has to stop running at some point. What if he is the best that will come her way? She thinks of the other men that she has had in her life, the earliest when she was only fourteen. She wouldn't go back, not even if she felt she had lost something valuable, to pick any of them up again. David is her natural path forward. He is her future. She turns to him and feels welcome and whole in his arms. She doesn't care that he could be breaking what is left of her spirit. Like old dry bread, she may as well be crumbling into little pieces, but she pushes herself deep, and even deeper into his arms.

Morning.
When Michal awakens, she feels like a woman who has found eternal youth or better days. She looks across the bed, crossing oceans of doubt, and finds David smiling back at her.

He closes his eyes, and tells her about the dream that he has had.

"I am in a great field, with all this green grass swaying in the wind. I feel like all the world is happy for me. Ain't no more questions. Even Solly can't touch me there. I see this young boy coming toward me; he can't be more than seven or eight years old. He's just walking toward me with this arrow in his hand.

"Johnnie has sent me,' the boy says to me. 'You must go.'

"Where?' I ask the boy.

"It doesn't matter,' he says, 'You must go far away from here. You must go quickly.'

"So I ask him, 'Is it really unsafe?' I mean, I want to know why I need to get the fuck up outa there.

"And get this, Michal. The boy says, 'Yes, but not for you.' Then he turns and walks away, still carrying this arrow in his hand."

Michal looks at David, wondering where he is going with this. He stares at her like he's questioning her sanity. "So, what do you think he meant?" he finally says.

"I don't know, David. I think I've got to get up from here and get dressed."

Laughing, he says, "Yeah, you're right. I'll run to Jackie's on the corner and get some eggs. I'm starving."

Later, when Michal and David get on the streetcar, they look around for a seat, as though just this once, the crowd will have decided not to go to work or school for this one day. The car jerks off, in a tinged, shuffling sound as it glides over the rails, singing out in not so gentle squeals. Michal is the first to notice that David's face is now glistening with sweat, though it is still the cooler hours of the day. She studies his face and becomes worried. He doesn't look back at her. His eyes appear to be locked on Mrs. Greedy, the old woman who rides the streetcar all day, and who now sits unnoticed and unheard until she sees David's eyes on her. This wakens her from a stupor-like silence, and suddenly she is throwing her story at David as though he is a catcher of words. Or at the very least that he will try to grab at some of the syllables that go flying by him. To Michal, he looks stunned: his body has slumped down so that his head is almost resting against his chest. The one arm that is not holding on to the pole in front of him is folded up so that the tips of his fingers touch his shoulder. It is as though he is trying to get his own attention.

"David!" Michal calls out to him. An instinctive type of fear has begun to crawl over her.

He doesn't answer.

Michal shakes him and grabs at the hand that clutches his shoulder. He doesn't appear to hear her. His eyes are locked on Mrs. Greedy. She talks on.

"You know my husband died in the same year that Big Bush went to war in Iraq," she says. "That's how I always remember it."

David says nothing.

"I've been alone since then. Well, all except for the Sisters at St. Mary's. Yes, they come and visit me every week. Mostly on Saturdays."

Nothing from David.

"You know I'll be seventy-one-years-old in December. I still got my own teeth though. Not many people can say that, can they?"

David's eyes are cold walls against the onslaught of her words.

"I just ride the streetcar 'cause I can meet people from all over the world. But you know, they get to meet me, too. I'm sure some of them go back to their county and tell their kinfolks about me."

Mrs. Greedy slows down then, perhaps seeing something in David's eyes that Michal and the other passengers do not. She jumps back when David leans to within inches from her face and says, "What if you were questioned on every fucking thing you do?"

Michal quickly pulls him away from the old woman.

"We all are, David." She is aware that she must talk him down and try to calm him back to himself, but it isn't working.

"All I know," he says, "is it's the year 20 fucking oh-8 and you'd think people had better things to do than fuck with me. I see more than they know."

"Yes, I know, David."

He ignores her. "I see them coming up the hill after me. I'm climbing, I'm climbing. It's a big-assed hill, and I can't get to the top with Solly pulling me down."

"What do you want me to do, David?" Michal thinks that if she keeps him calm, everything will be okay.

"I want you to get the fuck off me," he says.

Then he is standing so close to her that she feels his breath fall down on her in a shower of heated air.

At first, Michal doesn't believe his hands are wrapped around her neck—or that in the briefest of moments, David has finally and fully become someone else to her. He seems to want to silence her; as if doing so will stop the questions. She tries to grip at his arms, her nails cutting into his skin. Her head is back and her eyes feel as though they will fall to the floor. This is when she sees some of the people, who are now upside down, converging on them. Their hands arrive first, pulling at David, trying to force him to set her free. She feels the powerful slapping sounds that their bodies make as they try to tackle him. She feels the sweat on David's arm against her chest. An arm bumps her head. A foot lands on one of her legs. Through all of this, Michal does not hear a sound, as if the world has stopped speaking to her altogether. Before she loses consciousness, she thinks she hears David say, "Fucking Solly."

Michal opens her eyes, much later that day, and a nurse tells her that she is now a patient at "LSU, the old University Hospital."

Michal asks about David.

"The boy who tried to kill you?"

"Yes," she says tentatively, not wanting to believe her own words.

"He over here, too. Everybody talking about it. They found a tumor on this here side of his brain." But Michal has looked away and missed which side the nurse indicated. When Michal doesn't react, the nurse goes on: "Almost big as a mirliton, yeah. The doctors say it shoulda been something awful to go through."

Michal can't help but notice the way the nurse delights in telling her about David. It's as if her life's story has been added a new subplot, with David as the main character.

Michal wants to get out of this bed to see him for herself.

The nurse seems to understand her very thoughts, for she tells Michal, "His friend is with him. A tall boy, face kinda look like he been staying with white folks all his life."

"That would be Johnnie."

Michal feels relieved to hear this news, that David isn't alone, that Johnnie has been there to see him through this ordeal. She relaxes and allows an entire wall of tension to fall away from her.

"He never see a doctor?" the nurse asks.

"I think he did go, once, a little after Katrina, but you know how bad things were. He told me he sat around the Emergency room at one of those makeshift clinics. They didn't think a headache was all that serious."

The nurse just shakes her head. She tells Michal, "Don't worry yourself none, yeah. He'll be alright, now."

And Michal begins to think that perhaps they both will.

Drowning for Words

You once said that my eyes were the color of the deepest heart of the Mississippi. As I sit here in the attic, looking upon the roughly passing flood waters, I think of you in the same way that I thought of the sum of the condolences that came too late—with much sadness and anger and despair. But mostly, I wonder why you thought the color of my eyes could ever be compared to something like this. It is still early though. The sound the rain makes as it strikes this small window—it doesn't frighten so much as still me. The water came through the house so quickly. *Go*, you said. *There is water and canned food and an ax*. When I heard you say this to me, I knew that I should want to live. So much of me still didn't care. I needed to know who sentenced me to this place on earth without you.

My dear Charles, I had been dreaming of you. I was too frightened to sleep in our bed, so I stayed on the sofa last night. Sometime after midnight, I heard people walking the streets. *We can still make it to Jackson Barracks if we hurry*. I yelled out to a few of them, told them that the old military base would not offer any better protection than their own homes, that they were better off catching a ride downtown, to the Superdome if they could make it. No one seemed to listen, or to hear me, and I went back to the sofa. I listened as the wind caught pieces of tree limbs and sent the smallest, most insignificant items in our front yard tumbling across the street. I sunk my head deeper into the pillow, your pillow—the last one you bought. You always needed a firm place to lay your head. *A mind needs to be elevated*, you always said. It's true that you were a brilliant man, and you never had the kind of breathing problems older people sometimes get.

I lay for most of the night there on the sofa, fully awake, unable to close my eyes completely—with my hands crossed over my chest, ready for whatever finality the hurricane might bring. I had listened to Channel 8 most of the evening, hearing Bob Breck, in his comical way, say I should leave this place and find higher ground in some nearby state. What is my state of mind? I asked myself for some reason. The pun made me laugh, but I knew I should listen. You loved Breck, like he was some kind of weather god, or at least a newer version of Nash Roberts. Listening to Breck made me feel closer to you. My eyes drifted into a comforting darkness. The truth is that I didn't care to leave the only place where I still feel your presence.

I don't know why I am telling you all this. I know you'll not read any of these words. I hope someone else will. A last moment between us, even if you are there and I am here. The water has begun to rise again, though more slowly than before. Will it find closure here in the attic? If it does, where shall I go, Charles? You were wrong, there is no ax. I remembered just minutes after I found safety up here that you had taken it down last year—just before your accident, to finish off the small pine tree that Tropical Storm Lily had felled. I'm sure the ax is still somewhere in the back yard, among the pieces of firewood you chopped—unless the flood waters moved it.

I feel the wetness just beneath, soaking into the floorboards. I hear it slap and throw itself against the small door of the attic. I've used all the boxes of your clothes, the ones I stored up last year, refusing to give them to charity, like you would suddenly get up from your grave and come back to wear them. I pushed your old sweatshirts around the entrance to the attic—well, most of them. I saved the gray one, with the green lettering on it—Tulane. Didn't you wear it to every game? *Go, Green Wave!* you always shouted in my ear. I would turn away from you and patiently wait until you settled down again in the stadium seat. Oh, how I would love to hear one small cheer from you now. *Go, Evelyn!* you might say. *Don't give up even one breath!* And would I listen or turn away?

That's what I was dreaming about when the first of the water pushed on our beautiful house. It was as though the house was in the way of some larger, more powerful object. You know what I thought of? Large women who are so full-bodied that sometimes when they walk, they bump into other people by mistake. The smaller body can't help but give way. A small child, fall to the ground even. That's what it felt like, that first full gust of water that settled here. It frightened me into a wakefulness that I haven't been able to shake. I had been dozing off and on. My instinct was to go to the window and look out into the street, but when my bare feet touched the floor, they were immediately buried in water. *But the house is six feet off the ground*, you would probably say with astonishment. I lingered there, with my feet soaked, caught in a type of stupor that only scared, lonely people understand. Within moments, the water was at my knees.

That's when I heard your voice, Charles. It may as well have been the voice of Jesus because that's what it felt like to me. And I did carry myself as quickly as I could into the kitchen and then the hallway, where I gathered a chair and then pulled down the ladder to the attic. I could see nothing but darkness from where I stood. By then, the brown, ugly water had risen above my knees. I began my short climb into the dark pit above me. When my feet left the chair, I felt the water move it away, as though someone had suddenly decided to clear the hallway of debris. At one moment, I thought I would fall—and I would have, had I not thrown my elbow around a rung of the hanging ladder. I simply held on. I can't explain to you how quickly the water came into the house. Even there, as I struggled to pull myself into the attic, I began to think that it would not stop. I heard you say, *Evelyn, you're no spring chicken at sixty-seven, but you can get your ass up that ladder—now GO!* I forgot about water lapping at my feet and simply placed one foot up and then another. By then, all the contents of the house were being rearranged in a swirling ugly brownness. I looked down and saw your pillow floating into the kitchen.

I pulled myself into the attic and rested. The first thing I noticed was that neither of us had cleaned the one small compartment window since we'd lived here. There were many layers of dirt to wipe away before the darkened skies would come through, and even now the light only falls to the floor in awkward places, in little sheets and blankets of brightness. Then the wind turns upon the house again and the darkness falls and then lifts itself up like that heavyset woman, getting up from an old, bottomed out chair.

Why am I writing to you this way, in metaphors and similes? The writer in me wants to create, I suppose. For so many months the urge to write escaped me, all of those desires seeping out of me, like memories held too long. I suppose I knew that the only thing I wanted to write about was you, and how sad I am without you. *Stop feeling sorry for yourself*, you would say to me now.

I've been here in the attic for much of this one day, yet it feels like more days have passed. This is like looking out the one window of my own mind. I see what's going on around me, but I can hardly bear to watch it. Animals rush by, being carried along, their heads stretching out of the water. Lawn chairs float by like they've been expelled from a Lawn and Feed Store; someone could go into business for himself. Cars float slowly down our watered street. There was one—it was dark purple or black and looked like an ominous shroud approaching. I could not see if anyone was inside. Who would have been out driving at a time like this? What am I saying? It seemed as though the entire city was still on errands until the last possible moment. But now I think the current has simply stolen the vehicles. They bob and ebb, dancing in the water's rhythm.

And the water sings—it is happy to have found all this merchandise to carry. I wish it were a less sorrowful melody. You would think the water would roar as it courses through, the way it batters whatever it touches, its voice like a mighty lion in a wet jungle. It should be more like a cry, a weeping sadness for the job it must do. You always said, *Water is the great passageway—taking some to freedom, others to bondage.* I think of this now and wonder where, if anywhere, it will take me. I dread the full darkness of nightfall.

I've seen pieces of houses floating down the street. A chunky piece of someone's kitchen went by just now. The cabinets were all empty. I think of all the food that must be strewn along the way. Cans of salmon, I'd imagine. Your favorite breakfast: salmon with eggs and rice. Because you grew up in New Orleans, your tastes were so different than mine. And what about the rest of that house, the kitchen? Where is it now?

Charles, you and I never saw anything like this.

I feared what I had to do. First, let me tell you that the water leveled off for a few hours this afternoon. It even receded some. I was able to open the attic door and look down into the house. Plants and shoes and clothing sat atop the water like cream at the top of a glass of old milk. I had no idea how I would maneuver myself through it all, but I knew that I would find a way. As I sat here in the attic, it suddenly occurred to me that you and I had locked away our remaining valuables—those we had managed to save over the years after Betsy and Camille, and the flood of '95. Everything was in a small safe inside the chiffonier in our bedroom. There, I had also placed the journal I'd written. You jokingly called it *The Exodus*. You had said it sounded like a great departure of sorts. *Oh, look at the two people who have passed this way, and all the lessons they have learned!* I laughed with you, but I never told you that you were right. I had written about our new beginning, which could only have come from so many sad endings between us. It was about our survival over the years.

It wasn't until today, when it seemed lost to me forever, that I knew I must save our words, Charles. I had to go back into the water and pretend that it was filled with the sweetest manna from heaven. I would taste it and bathe in it if necessary, but I would save our story.

The water was cool on my legs as I lowered my body down from the attic. I was able to float immediately, and I began to push myself along with my arms and feet. I felt as though I were crawling through the water. I saw that something, the wind maybe, had broken out the windows. The outside light poured in. I knew the door had been pushed aside as well. Our house was no longer our own. A dead cat floated a small distance away from me, its fur caught on the edge of the stove's fan. Playthings from some family's yard bobbed up and down in the living room. I tried not to think about all the living things that could be in the water with me. Spiders and other creatures running across the water, on tiptoes.

When I neared our bedroom, I could see that the doorway was blocked by a large mass of furniture. I began to pull at the big settee that you had bought me for our 26th anniversary so many years ago. Surprisingly, it gave way easily and began to float down the hall in the opposite direction. I thought of mountains and how small they look when you drive away from them. I pulled on several smaller chairs, none of which seemed to belong to us. All of these things seemed to have found a common space to gather and ride out the storm.

At first, I thought our door was closed—although I couldn't imagine how it would have withstood the water's pressure. When I pulled the last chair away, I saw that there was a woman's body stuck at the top of the doorway. I thank God that her face was turned away from me. Even then, I jumped in fear. I let go of the chair that I had been attempting to pull away from the door. It floated back against the woman's body. For some reason, her legs were pinned beneath her, only the top of her thighs and torso floated above the dark, littered water. I could see that she was a rather large woman, or perhaps the water had bloated her into this shape. There were large air bubbles beneath the woman's clothes. I thought of life jackets that don't work.

Charles, I didn't know what to do then. It may as well have been a standoff. My instincts were to try and push the woman further into our bedroom. I don't know why—clearly, she could not lie on the bed until help arrived. I am sorry to say this, but it was at that moment that I remembered you never liked heavy-set women—their girth disturbed you somehow and you never found peace with it. Part of me hated you for even thinking such things. I knew I had to do something to preserve this woman's dignity. I couldn't just leave her there in that position. But slowly, I began to understand that I had no other choice. The only thing I could do was to try and get to the other side, inside the room, and claim the journal. I didn't want to turn back without it.

That's when I thought to dive under the woman and enter the bedroom from a lower position. I knew you wouldn't approve, but I've always been a good swimmer. I had no doubts that I could hold my breath for a few seconds until I was in the room. I grabbed my nose with one hand, lifted my other arm in the air, and then pushed off from the ceiling. I couldn't see very well and relied on touch. I followed the woman's legs downward, from her knees. I struggled to grab hold; for some reason I could go no further. Fear caught hold of me and forced me to let go. I shot back upward, coughing for air and spitting out that filthy water as soon as my head was out of the water.

There was nothing left to do in that moment but to allow the tears to come. They ran down my face and merged with the flood water. Oh, how I wanted to just give up then, to go back into the water and stay there with that woman. It occurred to me that it didn't matter, that you were gone and perhaps it was my time to go as well. I shed more tears. I was barely floating then—the strength in my legs was leaving me. I knew it would be easy to simply let go and sink down to the floor. I imagined that I could walk around down there until all the air finally left me. I could look for small children the woman might have been tugging to safety. Other people who might be in the water. I could push them all into the bedroom and sit with them on the bed; we'd all wait until rescuers came for us. I believe these thoughts are what brought me back to the reality I face here in our house: I will probably die here.

I knew instantly that I must forget about the journal, that even if I found it, it too would be lost—wet and soaking, beneath the dead brown water. I knew that I must get back to the safety of the attic and wait for any help that might come. I reached for the ceiling and attempted to walk with my hands, pulling my body back towards the ladder. As I rounded the corner, I saw that the dead cat was now loose from the stove's fan and was floating toward me. This small signal of death's impertinence did not frighten me. I looked back, as though I needed to see for one last time, the woman's bloated body still stuck at the entrance of our bedroom. I turned and moved on until I reached the ladder. I rested for a moment, then I pulled myself up the rungs once again. When I was safely in the attic, I closed the door and latched it shut. I was sure I would not open it again.

When I first came into the attic, I found a set of stationery you had given me for a birthday. I wondered why I had never used it. It was pretty enough. Pink flowers made a border around the edges, although pink was never a color I would choose. I had obviously felt cheated by you then, had likely asked why you chose that color. Looking at the stationery, I could see the way I'd taken you for granted. There were so many things you gave me, so many things you did for me that I simply disregarded. Isn't it the way of life to catch us sleeping when we should be awake? Seeing and understanding what is really there? Your dying in a car accident should have awakened me, or at least taught me that life is precious, and that even though you were no longer on this journey with me, I could still soar and be happy.

In these last hours, I am still writing. I've asked myself why I couldn't get beyond the woman downstairs—why I couldn't keep going until I reached the other side, where I knew the journal would be. I have no answer yet. Am I still afraid of what life will take away from me, even at this late, undeniable hour? I look out this tiny window, blurred by the rains that have come again. The water has come into the attic now. I wish for the ax that is not here. I wonder how long it will be until…I can't even say it, Charles. Downstairs, I was so ready to give up. And now? I want the world to know our story.

The Meeting

My grandmother's house is a place I often go to in my dreams—and sometimes I go there for real. The house sits bravely near the edge of an old country road; its only protection from the harsh world is a stout and mighty chinaberry tree that my grandfather must have planted over a hundred years ago. So, a while back, I'm invited to a meeting at my grandmother's house. When I walk in, I wonder if I should be there. I still feel like the child I had been so many years before, my soul aching as much as my body ever did, looking for my mother to comfort me after being hit in the head with one of those little green berries, hoping that she would just this once allow me to remain in the house with the grown folks, and not outside with those heathen children.

On this day, when I go to the meeting, I open the door and the front room is still the same—only it's winter now and a fire blazes quite genially in the fireplace. Over the mantel, the portrait of my grandmother and grandfather in their mid-lives hangs in just the way I remember it—my grandfather wearing his handsomeness like a badge across his broad chest and my grandmother leaning into her husband with one hand resting on his forearm. She also, in white, though now yellowed, and he in his one and only suit, now only a shade of black; it is the color of old death. Otherwise, the walls remain empty, like hospital rooms where the sick are expected to arrive soon.

I hear laughter and raucous conversation coming from the kitchen, which is the farthest room of the shotgun house, and I must walk through my grandparent's bedroom to get there. The voices carry through the thin walls, and I begin to recognize who some of the people are. I cannot mistake my grandmother's voice, which has always been deep but hollow like it flows through a thick tube of glass, and my mother's as well, which is just a more youthful version of my grandmother's. I hear my Aunt Sherry, who is still busy trying to boss my mother around, even after all these years. This makes me smile, and I briefly think of how terribly young we all were back then, even the grownups.

Then everything gets weird because I think I hear Oprah telling someone to let her sit up close, next to Jesus, and Coretta Scott King saying that if anyone is going to sit at the right hand of the Lord, it should be her. There are other voices mingled in, and to tell the truth, I can hardly wait to get to the kitchen to see what's really going on.

I open the door—now there's a door to the kitchen, but back in the old days, we just walked straight in—and have mercy, there is the Lord, my savior, Jesus the almighty, sitting at the head of this long table, you know the kind where you have to place an extension in the middle, only this extension is as wide, or wider, than the table itself; it's like somebody, my grandmother I imagine, had invited too many important people for dinner, expecting perhaps that not all of them would actually show up, but when they do, she has to keep lengthening the table to accommodate them.

As I look around the room, I realize that there has been an extra room added on, and this isn't the kitchen anymore but the dining room, and the kitchen is still beyond in a room added to the house. My grandmother sees me standing there all mystified and confused, and she lifts one hand and motions for me to come on in, and says, "Close that door behind you." She is standing, not sitting, just to the back and right of Jesus. She has on her apron and those same slippers that I remember her always wearing. My instinct tells me to run and hug her and give her an age-old kiss of greeting, but I see my mother, who I haven't seen in so many years, and I want to plant my eyes on her and leave them there, sure this time to follow her around so that she will not get away from me. It's true. When I see my mother sitting next to Alice Walker, of all people, I feel like I am finally home. I want to ask Alice to move over and let me sit next to my mother, but I know that's not going to happen, especially the way these women are arguing about who's sitting where. Briefly, I wonder how the seating was arranged, and more importantly, who made the guest list.

"You are late," my grandmother says to me, as if she is reading my state of mind and wants me to catch up with what's going on. "Take a seat there." She points to one of the two remaining seats.

"Hurry," someone says, "Don't let Satan try to steal his ass a seat." I realize it's Missy Elliott, who sits on the opposite side of the table across from Alice Walker, and next to my Aunt Sherry.

Everyone in the room nods their agreement, and their eyes tell me to sit down, quickly.

I can't help the befuddledness of my motions; I can barely move. Looking down the table at all these precious guests, well, it stills my heart. I may as well be a butterfly trying to land on each of their shoulders. I am floating in a moment in time, just holding on as best I can.

Jesus then speaks, and I think about true freedom, how none of us ever know how it feels. "I have looked forward to eating this meal with you," he says. "Let us pass the bread and divide it evenly among you."

So he breaks the loaf of bread and takes a small piece for himself and then passes the two larger pieces to the women sitting next to him, my first grade teacher, Mrs. Corning, on one hand and Zora Neale Hurston on the other. My teacher breaks off a piece and passes it on to Oprah, and Zora takes a piece and passes it on to Mrs. King. Oprah, to Aretha Franklin; Mrs. King, to my mother; Aretha, to my Aunt Sherry; my mother, to Alice Walker; Aunt Sherry, to Missy Elliott; and Alice, well, she has no one to pass the bread to unless she reaches over the empty chair and gives it to me, but Missy Elliott has already practically thrown the final, piddley piece that has come down that side of the table to me (this is that fresh version of Missy, when she first came out with a hit record). Alice and I look at Aretha and say nothing. Alice places half of her bread on the plate of the missing guest. I wonder if anyone, besides me, wants to know why my grandmother will not take her seat.

"I am to remain standing," she says, again, as if reading my mind.

"Who is greater," Jesus asks no one in particular, "the one who sits here at the table with you or the one who will serve you? Anyone who wishes to be first must be last. You must be the servants of all."

Before anyone can answer the riddle, my grandmother tells me to go and get the woman in the kitchen. I obey without asking the logical questions "Why?" or "Shouldn't I be here to discuss what Jesus has just proposed?" Never mind, I go.

As I am walking past Oprah, I hear her say to Aretha, "Perhaps we could get you to sing a song while we're waiting for the next guest to arrive." I don't hear Aretha's reply, but I must admit to myself, I would love to hear something off the *Amazing Grace* album or if that fails, her *Greatest Hits* will do.

When I open the door to this new kitchen, the one that has been added to my grandmother's house, seemingly just for this occasion, I see an aging black woman, in a maid's dark uniform with a white apron. She looks prematurely old, like life has beaten the shit out of her. She is bent over the stove, stirring something that is bubbling and leaving circles of steam floating up to her face. I wonder how my grandmother can suddenly afford a maid.

"Mmn, that's just about perfect," this woman says to me. She speaks as though she has known me all my life. "You know, it's your favorite: blueberry cobbler."

And even though I don't know this lady from Adam or Eve or any of their offspring, I suddenly want to ask her to be my new best friend.

"Don't worry about it," she says. "These things been decided long ago."

I ignore that last remark and remember why I've come. "My grandmother says for you to come there. Now." This part I add for emphasis, like I am in charge of this shindig.

"Oh, she did," the woman says.

"Yes, Ma'am." I have remembered my manners.

And the woman lays down her spoon and follows me, like I am Jesus petitioning his disciples. I look back, wondering how my cobbler is going to be finished. She hadn't even rolled out the crust yet.

She tells me, "It'll be alright. Don't worry."

When we get back to the other room, it seems as though every voice is raised in disagreement. I truly can't believe these women are behaving so rudely, in front of Jesus. It's like they have no faith in the system, no trust that things will be done to their satisfaction.

I hear my aunt, who never was one to wait, for anything, ask Aretha to sing, "Mary, Don't You Weep." But before Aretha can answer, my teacher, Mrs. Corning, says, "No, you know what I'd love to hear? 'Order My Steps.'" My teacher and I smile because we both know this is her favorite song in the world.

"That's not one of my songs, hon," Aretha says, dryly, like there's a big piece of bread stuck in her throat.

My teacher and I look at each other because we can't believe what we just heard. When did Aretha get particular about singing other people's songs? When did she stop being the Queen of all things lyrical? Our eyes tell each other to just let it go.

"I'll sing it," Missy Elliott says. "Missy be putting down on some church songs, chicky."

I don't know why, but I believe her and I'm all for having her try, but my grandmother and my mother, in unison, with emphasis, say, "No singing at the table."

I sit down in my seat at the opposite end from Jesus and wait. I see my grandmother talking to the woman I've just brought from the kitchen. Suddenly, the woman's face lights up. I swear, it's like she has turned ten shades brighter. Like Jesus has touched her and all her troubles have suddenly rolled away. She even begins to resemble someone I should know.

"Oh, Lord, Jesus, you done shown mercy on me." It's all she can say, as she looks over at Jesus. I know she wants to go to him and perhaps kiss his feet or bring him a glass of water—anything she could do to show her love for him. I see tears forming in her rich brown eyes, and I think that Zora could have created this woman in one of her novels. She is Phoebe perhaps, or Janie's grandmother, only before she got so old and gave out.

"Go on," my own grandmother says to the woman. "Take your seat at the table."

The woman walks slowly past Zora, Mrs. King, my mother, and Alice. When she arrives at the empty chair, she says, "This'll be the first time I been to a meeting inside a real house."

Instinctively, I know she means it's the first time she's been asked to come out of the kitchen and eat. Part of me wants to cry, too, because I'm all soft and warmhearted like that, but also because I know exactly how the woman feels. This is the first time I've been allowed to eat with the likes of these magnificent women, especially since my grandmother and my mother and my teacher and my aunt passed on over. They just don't make people like them anymore. That's when it hits me that I am the special guest, that these aren't people my grandmother would likely meet up with in heaven. These are people brought here for me. And then, I surely want to cry. I want to lie down on the floor and bawl like a baby, only there'd be no kicking and screaming, just calm, dedicated tears rolling off my happy face and onto the well-worn floor.

Where do we go from here? I ask myself.

Zora says, "Who's going to wrassle us up something to eat? Y'all know I like to cook; just don't expect me to keep a tidy kitchen."

"I'll do it," my mother says. And no one dislikes the idea because they all know she can throw down on some vittles. Even my aunt doesn't object.

But Jesus stops them all. "Have you so little faith?" he asks. "I fed thousands with two fish and five loaves of bread. Haven't we more than that here on the table?"

We all take a look, and sure enough, there are apples and pears and jam and butter and another loaf of bread and some kind of cheese that's been hardly touched. But just to make sure, we look at Aretha and wait for her agreement.

"Don't look at me," she almost sings, her round cheeks next to bubbling. "Ree knows how to make do."

"I believe you do," Mrs. King says. I'm surprised at her tone because it's almost flippant, like she might still be questioning the friendship Aretha and her husband had so many years ago.

My teacher, perhaps from years of knowing how to break up a clash of characters, turns the attention back to Jesus. "Teacher," she calls him, "I was wondering what message you'd like to leave with us before you go."

He's going? We haven't even eaten yet.

"The greatest of the commandments never changes," he says. "Love God, our father, above all, and then love your neighbor as you love yourself."

"Amen," Oprah says. "That's the message I try to put out every day. It's my ministry. I believe that if we can all just learn to take care of one another, this world will be a better place. Don't you?"

"Yes, Ma'am," my aunt says. "Satan will surely test you."

"Yes, Mrs. Sherry, you're right," Oprah returns, but before she can carry on with this little sanctified discussion with my aunt, my mother stands up and clicks her spoon on her water glass.

"Excuse me," she says. "You all have been wonderful to come here today and spend this time with my daughter." And looking at Jesus, "The Lord knows, I thank you."

Jesus nods his head. Everyone else clears their throats and says things like, "Oh, that's alright. We're glad to do it" and "Don't mention it, none" and "No, no, thank you for having us." And as they say these things, they look at my mother and then they look at me, as if to say, "Yes, we mean you, too."

My mother continues her speech, and for some reason I think she's about to start off on a tremendously long monologue. This can't be true, though, because Jesus is pulling out his chair, preparing to stand.

"The Lord is my Shepherd; I shall not want," my mother begins. And Jesus sits back in his seat.

My mother continues: "Those was words my mother always told me to say whenever I was in trouble or when I was about to take a trip or even for good times when things was good. And when I got married and had chirren of my own, I told them to repeat the 23rd Psalm." Then she looks at me. "No matter how bad things get, you can always count on the Lord."

"I do," I say. I can't help but break in. "I do, Momma. I do."

"Then I did my job right," she says.

By the time she says these last words, she and I both have tears streaming down our faces. I am that child again, wanting to run into her arms and find sweet solace. And that's when I know it's just a dream, that if I walk over to her standing there, only her spirit will be waiting, and that part of her I cannot touch, at least not physically, so that I can feel it, wrap myself in it.

She and my grandmother give each other a hug then, as though they have just met each other after a long, difficult absence. They are so glad to be with each other. My mother's stout self wraps her arms around my grandmother's frail frame, and in my heart I want my mother to remain there where I know she'll be happy.

Jesus says, "Surely, I am with you always, even till the end of all ages. Now, I must surely go." To me specifically, he says, "Take everything you have and use it. Remember that all things are possible."

That's when my eye catches the true knowledge of the woman sitting next to me, this woman whom I have brought from the kitchen to eat this special dinner with us. She is my friend, Glenda, from so many years ago. She has reportedly lived a miserable life, touched specifically by the cruelties of life after she caught a terrible disease. Only a few years before, I had learned that she'd died, almost unrecognizable to those who'd known her. She had been poor and had chosen to take a seat at the back of every table in life, never wanting to be a hindrance to anyone. Somehow, in my long journeys, I had forgotten her and had carried on with my life without looking back to search for her. Seeing her there now, at this table with me, even in my dreams, I know I've been given that chance to say goodbye.

"No need," she says to me. "Don't worry about it. The cobbler's in the oven."

With that, Jesus rises and goes from the room, saying, "Peace be with you."

Does it suddenly feel like Christmas to anyone else?

I would like to say that when Jesus left, all the women continued to behave themselves, but you see Zora was there and she said, "All right, y'all, let's spread some jenk and have a good time."

And even my Aunt Sherry liked that idea. Suddenly, there were Chippendales in their tights and bowties bringing out bowls and bowls of cobbler and bottles of Cristal; no, I mean Brut champagne.

"Break me off," Missy Elliott said, flashing her gold, and I knew she liked this idea. Pretty soon, my grandmother's house wasn't a sad and lonely place at all.

Acknowledgments

I thank God for his love and mercy.

I thank my family: Venesta, Sampson, Laura, Hattie (in absentia), Gloria, Lacey, Joseph, Trea, and Shanice for the laughter and the unconditional support.

I thank my BFF Del for encouraging me always, and Gretchen for being such a great reader.

I thank my dear cousins and extended family for their friendships, and my church family for helping me find spiritual peace.

I thank Dave and Bruce for their patience and guidance in putting this book together.

I thank the University of New Orleans and Spalding University's MFA in Writing Program, especially my mentors Randy and Richard, and each of the instructors and fellow writers who helped me develop as a writer.

I thank all my students and my colleagues at Our Lady of Holy Cross College, especially Claudia and Phyllis, for their encouragement and the many opportunities to read these stories.

I thank all the writers who I have studied over the years, from Hurston, Morrison, and Walker to Kafka, Wolff, and Ha Jin – writers like Kincaid, who helped me see sentences, Marquez, who gave me magical realism, and Gaines, of course, for writing about Louisiana as it is.

Printed in Canada by Imprimerie Gauvin.